THE PERSUASION OF MISS KATE

BOOK FOUR
MY NOTORIOUS AUNT
A HUMOROUS TRADITIONAL REGENCY

KATHLEEN BALDWIN

What critics say about The Notorious Aunt Series:

Lady Fiasco:

"Tyrell and Fiona's journey from desire to deep and lasting emotion makes Kathleen Baldwin's romance enjoyable."

– Romantic Times

"A winning mix of wit and humor. Baldwin makes delightful mischief in her debut Regency romp."

– Elisabeth Fairchild, RT Lifetime Achievement Winner

Mistaken Kiss:

"Kathleen Baldwin evokes some very tender moments as Willa learns that love will find a way in this warm and charming tale."

– Romantic Times 4½ Stars

"...a delight... laughter aplenty... sparkling dialog that left me with a smile on my face. I highly recommend this engaging Traditional Regency." *– Cheryl Sneed, Rakehell Reviews*

"I love these "Aunt Honore" books and this one does not fail. ... I really enjoyed this sweet story and the wonderful characters."

– Clean Romance Reviews

Cut from the Same Cloth:

"...a charming book, with the lightness and freshness of a sunny day in the park." *– Yvonne Choi, Rakehell Reviews*
"...believable characters with realistic traits, humor, and a bit of danger to create a wondrous painting that will linger in your mind's eye long after you finish the story. Terrific!"

– Detra Fitch, Huntress Reviews, 5 stars

"...a humorous and enchanting tale with intrigue and danger"

– Romantic Times, 4 Stars

What critics say about the Stranje House Novels

"**A School for Unusual Girls** is enticing from the first sentence . . . Baldwin has an ear for period dialogue as she draws us into this world of sharp, smart young ladies who are actually being trained and deployed for the British war effort by the mysterious headmistress, Miss Stranje. It's speculative historical fiction, with a trace of steampunk inventiveness."
— *New York Times Sunday Book Review*

"Sign me up for Kathleen Baldwin's *School for Unusual Girls*. It sucked me in from the first few pages and kept me reading until late into the night." —**Meg Cabot**, #1 NYT-USA *Today* bestselling author of *The Princess Diaries*

"Spellbinding! A *School for Unusual Girls* is a beautifully written tale that will appeal to every girl who has ever felt different . . . a true page-turner!"
–Lorraine Heath, NYT-USA *Today* bestselling author

"I enjoyed this story immensely and I closed my kindle with a satisfied sigh." —YA Insider on *Exile for Dreamers*

"(Readers) seeking period romance with a twist need look no further." —**Kirkus** on **Exile for Dreamers**

"An outstanding alternative history series entry and a must-have for teen libraries." —School Library Journal

"**Refuge for Masterminds** moves at a fast pace from the first page and doesn't stop. Although it is written with a young adult audience in mind, it is a fun and enjoyable novel and will also appeal to adult readers." —Historical Novel Society

"I am in love with the Stranje House novels. Seriously, in love."
—Book Briefs

Books by
Kathleen Baldwin

THE MY NOTORIOUS AUNT SERIES:
HUMOROUS REGENCY ROMPS

LADY FIASCO
MISTAKEN KISS
CUT FROM THE SAME CLOTH
THE PERSUASION OF MISS KATE

EXCITING ALTERNATE HISTORY SPY SERIES FOR TEENS
FROM TORTEEN/MACMILLAN
(SET IN THE REGENCY ERA)

THE STRANJE HOUSE NOVELS:

A SCHOOL FOR UNUSUAL GIRLS
EXILE FOR DREAMERS
REFUGE FOR MASTERMINDS

A REGENCY NOVELLA
THE HIGHWAYMAN CAME WALTZING

CONTEMPORARY TEEN FANTASY
DIARY OF A TEENAGE FAIRY GODMOTHER

A HUMOROUS TRADITIONAL REGENCY

The Persuasion of Miss Kate

BOOK FOUR
MY NOTORIOUS AUNT

Kathleen Baldwin

INK LION BOOKS

First Edition April 2021

Printed in the United States of America

0 9 8 7 6 5 4 3 2 1

To all of you who have set aside your wants and desires so that you could care for others. May God pour out His richest blessings on you.

Chapter 1
Death to All Roses

"I'M DONE FOR."

Snip.

A withered blossom dropped into Kate's gardening basket. "He's sealed my fate—the wretch!"

Snip. Snip.

"No help for it now. I'm going to be an old maid, and that's all there is to it." She paused and stared at the murderous shears in her hand. "Two and twenty." She moaned. "I shall be on the shelf forever." Kate clipped off another dying rose. "A spinster," she said accusatorially to the shears.

The gardening shears had the good grace to remain mute.

Spinster. She grimaced.

This time a perfectly formed pink rose, barely open, fell prey to her clippers. She'd come to the garden intending to remove the dead roses. Except now, it seemed only fitting that the annoyingly perfect bud should be cut off before its prime. That's what Greyson had done to her. Ruined her life. Cut her down before she'd had a chance to truly bloom.

The scoundrel!

Snip.

Another fresh bloom met its doom and fluttered helplessly into her basket. Kate's grip on the pruning shears tightened. Her teeth clamped together, and she went at it. Her blade lopped heads off roses with the fury of a soldier in battle. Along with withered flowers that deserved removal, she beheaded ripe full blooms, as well as newly opened ones.

Clipped them all.

Why should they have a chance to bloom? She didn't.

Kate came to an unopened white bud and hesitated. Something about the fresh white petals innocently peeking out between the seams reminded her of her younger sisters.

Her shoulders slumped, and the snippers nearly slipped from her drooping hand. She couldn't bear the thought of her sisters never having a chance at happiness. The whole family would bear the shame of it now, and it would be all her fault for not holding her tongue.

No! She shook her head. The fault was Greyson's—*except she swore then and there that she would never call him by his given name again.* Never. It brought up too many fond memories. No, indeed, this whole situation was the high-and-mighty Lord Colter's fault. It was he who ought to be dismembered, not defenseless roses. How dare he renounce their engagement?

The scoundrel.

What's more, he'd had the unmitigated gall to call her a shrew.

A *shrew!*

And he did so in front of everyone—the *entire village.*

It would've been humiliating enough if he'd said it on the street. But did the black-hearted devil choose so private a place as a village street? Oh, no. Lord Colter was not nearly so considerate as that. He hurled his shaming diatribe at her right in the middle of the ballroom floor, in full view of everyone at the Clapsforth-on-Wye Assembly Ball.

How dare he stop dancing and read her a piece of his mind? *During* the cotillion. Other dancers froze in place. The musicians screeched to a halt. Mrs. Oates squawked as if she'd been slapped. Mr. Peterson, Master of Ceremonies, gasped and his staff clattered to the floor.

"Heavens!" Lady Plimpton covered her outburst with her fan, eyes wide as an owl's at midnight.

All heads turned in their direction.

Everyone heard him.

Everyone.

Of course they did. Lord Colter had scolded her loud enough for folks in the next county to hear. Not a soul in Clapsforth-on-Wye missed his scathing condemnation. And what did he say? *Oh my!* What fine, saintly words he spilled over her head?

"Fine words, indeed." She jabbed the blades at another hapless rose and mimicked his irritated tone. "For pity's sake, Kate. Must you carp at me on every turn?"

Then came the *coup de grâce*, the stab to her heart.

Lord Colter announced to one and all, "I would rather rot in hell than suffer ten more minutes in your company."

The tip of her shears trembled slightly. How dare he say such a thing?

Was she really that terrible?

Maybe.

Curse her tongue.

Why must she always spout exactly what she was thinking? Papa had cautioned her a dozen times to mind her tongue. Except he must shoulder at least part of the blame because he always laughed at her witticisms. *Laughed.* Great galloping belly-shakers. When he really ought to have scolded her.

Snip.

The decapitated blossom dared to tumble off the edge of her basket and fall to the ground.

Imagining the ruddy thing was Lord Colter, Kate stomped on the fallen rose. *Hard.* So hard that one of the thorns pierced her kid slipper. She hopped back from the assaulting flower, her chest heaving with indignation.

"Enough!" she shouted at the infuriatingly blue sky. Where were storm clouds when she needed them? She grabbed a handful of the wretched blooms in her basket and hurled them into the air. If only they were spears that would fly straight into Lord Colter's cold, rotten heart, piercing it the way he'd pierced hers.

Except that wasn't true.

Kate was made of sterner stuff than that. He hadn't broken her heart. Not really.

Oh, she'd liked him well enough. Of course she did.

Didn't she?

Why else would she have agreed to marry him two years ago? They'd been friends since they were children, and although she disliked admitting it, looking at Greyson sometimes made her stupid heart beat a tiny bit faster. After all, he had a pleasant enough appearance, if one liked that revoltingly masculine type. His jaw was a trifle too imperious for her taste. And that over-bearing Roman nose—why would anyone like a nose like that? Not to mention his height. How many times had she strained her neck looking up at him?

Never mind all that.

Kate was immune to his charms.

She took a deep breath. All in all, her heart remained intact. That discovery surprised her. Rather than being broken, it seemed to pump stronger than ever. No, it was her reputation the villain had shattered.

And why had he shattered it? A *trifle*.

A perfectly innocent remark or other—she could scarcely remember what. She may have mentioned he looked as if he hadn't shaved that morning. Oh, yes, that was it. And on the next turn of the dance, she mentioned that he ought not neglect such matters as others might consider him careless of his appearance.

She may have offered him one or two more pieces of advice before running afoul of his temper. All perfectly sound observa-tions. And for that, he'd accused her of merciless henpecking.

Henpecking.

Folderol. She was merely concerned with his well-being. He had no right to turn on her like a great snorting bull. Yet he did. And she'd jolly well like to rip out his gizzard for it.

Kate flung another handful of spears at her invisible foe, wishing one of the stems would fly the short distance to his neighboring estate and poke him in the eye. Instead, one of the thorny stems stabbed her finger.

Drat.

She sucked the puncture and surveyed her handiwork. White and pink petals lay strewn across the green lawn as if thrown for a bride.

A bride.

Rose petals would never be scattered for her.

Not now.

Not ever.

No one would want her now. Not after he'd exposed her character to half the world. Not that it mattered. Marriage only meant more work anyway. Then again, she didn't bargain on shouldering this humiliation for the rest of her life, either.

Ruination.

Drat his black heart!

The basket slid from her arm. Her hands fell limp at her sides. Kate's throat tightened, and she felt an utterly foreign sensation—an uncomfortable quickness of breath and a quivering in her chest. Water welled up in her eyes. Then the unthinkable happened. Something she'd forbidden herself to do ever again. *Ever.* Not since her mother died had Kate given way to a single tear.

Not one solitary drop.

But now, unless she missed her guess, she was about to cry.

Oh no.

She couldn't.

She mustn't.

Nevertheless, water leaked from her eyes, stinging, blazing an acidic trail down her cheeks. Her nose stuffed up, and . . . *sweet lambs of spring!*

There was more. A keening noise burst from her throat. She couldn't stop it. The more Kate tried to restrain it, the more fiercely it exploded into an ear-shattering wail.

Battle lost—she dropped to her knees and let herself sob. Her shoulders shook in uncomfortable heaves for only a few moments.

One by one, she gathered up all the poor spilled roses, weeping tears over every murdered bloom, carefully scooping up each fragile velvety petal, and gently laying them to rest in her basket.

Each one a tragedy.

Each one a lost hope.

When she finished, Kate blotted her eyes on the corner of her apron. She fanned the air with her hand to cool her cheeks. She mustn't allow her sisters to see her like this. *Weak.*

I am not weak.

She couldn't afford to be weak.

Kate had to think of her sisters. Her humiliation cast an ugly shadow over all of them. If they hoped to weather this public indignity, they would need to remain brave and stalwart.

There was no time to dwell on *her* lost future. She stood and brushed off her skirts, determined to demonstrate courage so that her sisters would be able to navigate the tricky waters ahead and secure suitable husbands for themselves. She set the garden tools by the back door and slipped off her pattens. Treading quietly through the kitchen, to the parlor, she considered the future of each of her younger siblings.

Dear sweet Nora was next to Kate in age, and just turned seventeen. A pretty girl, but too quiet, always preoccupied with concerns about something or someone else. Nora was completely oblivious to the yearning looks she received from the young men in the village. Now that Kate's life was a hopelessly closed book, she would turn her attention to finding a suitable match for Nora.

Then there was Sadie.

Kate sighed.

Sadie would turn fifteen in November and was already more trouble than a bushel full of barn cats. Sadie churned out mischief faster than fresh cream could be made into butter. *Willful little minx.*

And then, there was the youngest—Mama's surprise baby, Matilda.

Tilly.

Precocious little Tilly, only ten, but cleverer than all of them put together. Kate had been there at her birth. In those last dreadful moments, as blood poured from Mama's body and her skin turned whiter with each passing second, she had pressed the wee little bundle into Kate's arms.

"Take care of her, my darling. I'm so sorry. So very sorry." Mama's eyes had flooded with grief. "Take care of your sisters, but, darling, you must remember . . . remember to . . ."

To do what?

Kate would never know what else her mother had intended to say. She'd reached for Kate's cheek, but Mama's fingers had only fluttered briefly against her skin, like the faint brush of a falling leaf.

Her mother's passing left a hole in Kate's heart. A dark, frightening hole—if she were to admit it. A hole growing into an ever-widening chasm that no one could fill—not her father, not Lord Colter, nor her sisters—a swirling sea of anger, pain, resentment, and a hundred other sins.

Kate shook her head at her errant thoughts. *Mustn't dwell on that.* She had no right to be angry.

Dying wasn't her mother's fault. It was a common enough thing to happen in childbirth. *There*—that was a blessing she ought to count. As a spinster, Kate would be spared the dangers of bearing children.

She headed to the parlor, dragging her fingers along the wall. Nearly to the door, she slowed her steps, listening to her sisters talking conspiratorially.

"He's not going to eat it." Nora sounded upset. "This won't work."

Tilly plunked an F-sharp on the pianoforte. "Did you put enough bacon grease on it?"

Bacon grease?

Kate waited outside the door, trying to figure out what they were up to before entering.

Sadie answered Tilly's odd question. "I most certainly did. I even stuck a piece of ham between the pages."

"Well, it's not working," Tilly complained.

"I can see that," Sadie snapped. "Ralphie, no! Don't lick it. Take a bite." The aged spaniel whined gloomily in response. "Come on, old boy," she coaxed. "Eat it! There's a good lad."

Kate heard the familiar swish-swish of her sister scuffing

against the floorboards. Nora must be pacing, a nervous habit she'd acquired as of late. "Maybe we should hide it."

"That won't do." Sadie argued. "We need to make it unreadable."

Kate leaned closer to the doorway. *What can they be doing?* She knew from experience that if she barged in now and demanded an explanation, the three of them would shut their lips tighter than clams at low tide.

"I don't think Ralphie likes paper." Nora sounded distressed.

"Nonsense. He used to chew up our books, didn't he?" Tilly was right, although how the child could remember that far back mystified Kate.

"He was a puppy then," Nora argued. "It's been years since he chewed up so much as a slipper."

"Open wide, Ralphie." Sadie stopped trying to sweet-talk their faithful spaniel and, despite the dog's whimpers of resistance, took a firmer approach. "Do your duty. This is for Kate."

For me?

The pianoforte bench scraped against the floorboards, and Tilly pattered over to the dog. "Maybe he objects to Aunt Honore's scent. Cousin Fiona warned us that our aunt is a rather unreliable lady, and I hear dogs are sensitive to such things."

Nora sighed softly. "*Unscrupulous* might be a more apt description of our dear aunt's character."

True. Kate had read the society columns and heard accounts from their cousins. Aunt Honore's friends were the crème de la crème of high society, but wherever the Lady Alameda went, scandal was sure to follow.

"Worse." Sadie's wry tone echoed down the hall. "Everyone knows Aunt Honore is mad as a hatter. Which is precisely why we can't let Kate read this letter."

Letter?

To me! Kate had heard enough. Her sisters were trying to destroy something that belonged to her. She took a step, prepared to burst into the room, but stopped when Nora said, "Papa meant well, I'm sure. But he should never have told his sister what happened to our Katie."

Kate reeled back and pressed against the wall. He wouldn't have, would he? Did he tell Aunt Honore about Lord Colter jilting her? Why would he spread the tale of her humiliation?

Oh, Papa! How could you?

"What was he thinking to suggest Lady Alameda should take Kate to London? The very idea is unthinkable." Sadie sounded ridiculously pious and grown-up, a perfect imitation of the gossipy matrons of Clapsforth-on-Wye.

Kate tapped her fingers against the wall. *Was it unthinkable?*

"If only Lady Alameda was a fit guardian." Nora's voice, normally so soothing and sweet, conveyed a ridiculously parental tone. "But she isn't. Especially not with Kate's present state of mind. You saw her in the garden. Poor thing is rather up in the boughs. And we all know the London season is full of pitfalls around every bend. Without proper guidance, our Katie is bound to make a muddle of things inside of a week."

Proper guidance?

A muddle.

Kate's fist turned into mallets. What did Nora know about

London? Nothing except what she read in the papers. London was
. . .

London!

Far away from here.

Kate pushed away from the wall. She could escape Clapsforth-on-Wye. What did her sisters think they were doing meddling with her future? She spun into the room with all the fury of a typhoon.

Nora jumped back from the hearth, where she and Sadie had been kneeling beside Ralphie. She snatched her embroidery up from a chair and held it in front of herself as if that frail bit of cloth and needlework might protect her.

Sadie tugged the letter out of Ralphie's mouth and hid it behind her skirts.

"There you are!" Tilly smiled as if genuinely happy to see Kate, then her eyes widened. "Uh-oh. You overheard us, didn't you?"

Kate was too furious to answer. Instead, she thrust her hand out to Sadie in a wordless demand for her rightful property.

Sadie grimaced, but slowly acquiesced, handing over the rumpled parchment dripping with bacon fat and dog drool. She had the audacity to point at Tilly and say, "It was her idea."

"It was." Tilly admitted unapologetically. "We *had* to do something."

"Get. Me. A. Cloth," Kate ordered through gritted teeth.

Sadie raced to the kitchen to retrieve a cleaning rag. Kate shook the tattered, sodden letter at Nora. "*You* should've known better."

Nora bowed her head, slid into the chair, and hunkered over

her embroidery, stitching intently.

"And I am *not* up in the boughs." Kate mopped Ralphie's drool from the parchment, careful not to smear any more ink than what was already splotched and smudged. She smoothed out the tooth marks and tried to decipher what was left of her aunt's mangled missive. Although barely legible, she could scarcely believe her good fortune. Her aunt really did intend to bring her to London.

She finished reading and glanced up at her sisters. "You didn't read it all the way through, did you?"

Nora shook her head.

Sadie sniffed and puckered her lips as she always did when justifying her rash behavior. "The first part was alarming enough. We thought it best to destroy it before—"

"Before you knew what the rest of the letter contained?" Kate shook her head. "It's a lucky thing Ralphie didn't eat it. If he had, we would not have known Lady Alameda is due to arrive on the morrow."

"What?" Nora swallowed. "She's coming here?"

"Yes. So, we'd best prepare, don't you think? Our aunt, *a countess*, plans to take luncheon with us and then remove with me to London for the season."

Far away from Lord Colter.

Away from this wretched village.

And, for once in my life, away from my responsibilities.

"As you consider yourself able to decide what is best for others . . ." Kate glanced pointedly at Nora, "in my absence, I shall leave the running of father's household to you."

"That's not what I meant—"

"Oh, I rather think it is. You clearly believe yourself more capable of navigating the hazards of London society than I am. If that is so, you ought to have no trouble at all managing things here in quiet little Clapsforth-on-Wye."

"I never said . . ." Nora's mouth opened and shut with possible retorts, blinking helplessly as if she didn't know which way to leap. "I didn't mean . . ."

Sadie's lips remained buckled tight. She sat petting Ralphie while carefully contemplating the stones on the fireplace as if they hadn't been there since Queen Elizabeth's reign.

Scheming, no doubt.

It was Tilly who finally found a clear-headed voice. "You can't leave us." The child's brow crumpled, and for a moment, Kate felt her escape narrowing down to a pinhole. Then Tilly thrust her chin out at a shockingly stubborn angle. Her eyes fairly burned with willfulness. "I won't let you."

"Try and stop me." The words sprang from Kate's mouth before she'd thought them through, but if it came to a war of wills with a ten-year-old, Kate intended to win.

_Chapter 2
The Aunt Cometh

THE NEXT DAY, Kate worried her sisters might be right.
Going to London with her aunt could prove a disaster. The
prudent thing would be to stay home. Realistically, though,
would stumbling into a new catastrophe be any worse than her
current situation here in Clapsforth?

No.

Ergo, it is worth the risk.

Now then, back to business. Kate tapped her cheek as she
went over her plans for her luncheon with Aunt Honore. She'd
asked the cook to make a starter of *Soupe à la Flamande*. Not
Kate's favorite, but creamed vegetables seemed more sophisticated than their usual fare of chicken broth. For the main course,
she would serve roasted partridges alongside curried parsnips
and rice, and fresh bread and wine, followed by cheese and baked

pears. It was extravagant for a midday meal at their house, but by Lady Alameda's standards, no doubt it would appear humble. There hadn't been time to hire a footman. Agnes, their housemaid, would have to serve.

Kate untied her apron and smoothed out her day gown. Now, where had her sisters gotten off to?

The scamps claimed they were taking a stroll to visit Mr. Treadwell, the village bookseller, and meekly promised to return in time to greet their aunt. Kate wasn't a fool. They were up to something.

No *matter*. The table looked beautiful, and Kate's trunks were packed and ready to load onto her aunt's coach. Whatever nonsense her sisters were plotting, she would not let it stop her from leaving. This opportunity afforded her the only chance of being anything other than her father's spinster housekeeper. Speaking of father, it was time to extract him from his study.

Kate tiptoed in and cleared her throat. "I expect your sister to arrive at any moment, Papa."

He lifted one finger. "Yes, yes. I'll only be a moment longer." He sat at his desk, bent over the account books as always. In all likelihood, Sir Linnet was the most frugal squire in the whole of England. Kate respected his attention to detail. It served them well and kept his mind occupied. Although he accompanied his daughters whenever duty required, he didn't have much use for society and had never shown a desire to remarry.

At last, when he finally emerged from his study, he came and stood beside Kate. "Ah!" He clapped his hands together. "The table looks splendid. Your aunt will be impressed."

"Thank you, Papa. I hope it is fine enough for her." Kate

doubted it. Aunt Honore was frightfully rich and accustomed to the luxuries of town. Kate had heard tales of the excesses and wonders of London. She could scarcely wait to see the place for herself.

Papa put his arm around her shoulders. "Your Aunt Honore won't care so much about the finery. It's your company that will interest her. Mind you, not in the ways you might expect. When it comes to people, my sister is . . . um . . . how shall I put this? Something of an original in her preferences. Watch your step with her, child, and your, er, your tongue."

"I will, Papa."

He clasped Kate's shoulders tighter for a moment, let go, and immediately set to pacing exactly the way Nora did when distressed. "Oh, bother. Now that I consider the realities, I'm wondering if this is the right thing to do. I'd thought after the, uh . . . the incident, that you might be more comfortable in different surroundings." His thick gray eyebrows pinched together in worry.

She gave his sleeve an affectionate tug, straightening his cuff. "You were quite right, Papa. I'm looking forward to a change of scenery. Visiting London is just the thing. I shall ask Aunt Honore to take me to Astley's and the opera. Perhaps she'll take me on a tour of London Tower." It relieved Kate to see his face relax.

He chuckled at her enthusiasm. "Doesn't seem much like you, Katherine, to play the tourist. But if it makes you happy, then all is well and good." He glanced out the window. "Ah. Here come your sisters dilly-dallying up the road. Unless I miss my guess, they're up to something."

"Agreed. The little minxes look far too cheerful." Kate crossed her arms like a general surveying the battlefield. "Don't let it worry you, though. I'm equal to whatever they've got tucked up their sleeves."

He chucked her under the chin as if she were twelve again. "That's my girl. Always with your chin up and your face to the wind."

The way he said it made Katherine feel as if she were braving a terrible storm or some deadly disease instead of the pitying looks of her neighbors and the patently false commiserations from the other girls in the village. Of course, there was the prospect of her impending spinsterhood.

Even so, it could be worse.

Much worse.

What if she were a destitute crippled orphan with a bad case of the plague. *Quite right.* Whatever happened from here on out, she would remember things could always be worse. That would be her new motto in life.

Sadie skipped past the dining room looking altogether too innocent, and Tilly followed her wearing a positively triumphant expression. Nora shuffled in last. "The table looks beautiful." She said in greeting but avoided eye contact.

Kate's arms remained crossed. She called after them. "Do hurry and change out of your street clothes. Aunt Honore will be here any minute."

An accurate prediction.

Not five minutes later, a large black coach, pulled by a matched team of four, with the unmistakable De Alameda crest emblazoned on the side, clattered up the road to the house and stopped. The footman climbed down from his perch, lowered the coach steps, and opened the coach door. Kate watched from the window, holding her breath. Their notorious aunt stepped out, garbed entirely in funeral black as if a newly made widow.

Kate clutched her father's arm. "I thought her husband died years ago?"

"He did," Papa answered, sounding as baffled as Kate.

"Did someone else in the family die recently?"

"Not to my knowledge." Papa rubbed the back of his neck. "Unfortunately, with my sister, there's no accounting for her attire. All that black"—there were yards and yards of it—"may mean someone dear to her died, or it might mean she's simply in a mournful mood." He swallowed hard. "As I said, watch your step."

He continued to mutter his reservations about sending Kate to stay with his impetuous sister even as he strode to the door to offer the lady a warm greeting. Arm in arm, they came into the sitting room. He did not stand on ceremony. He smiled broadly and gestured to his daughter. "This is my Kate."

Kate curtsied with as much dignity as she could muster, but upon rising, her aunt embraced her as she would a beloved niece, rather than a girl she'd merely patted on the head on two other occasions.

"My poor girl! *Poor* dear," Aunt Honore gushed. "You must be beside yourself. What a terrible tragedy. My deepest condolences."

"For . . .?" Kate asked with genuine confusion. Surely, her aunt wasn't referring to the *incident*.

Except she was.

The pity in her aunt's expression along with the raised eyebrows confirmed it.

"Oh, *that*." Kate stepped back. "I assure you, Aunt. I am not indisposed in the least." She waved away the lady's sympathy as if it were an annoying gnat. "On the contrary, may I offer *you* my condolences? You are in deep mourning. Pray, who passed from this mortal coil?"

Lady Alameda huffed loudly. "Mortal coil, *shmortal* coil." She yanked off the black headpiece that held her mourning veil and tossed it onto a chair. "I wore all this on your account." She wheeled on her brother. "You said she was distraught. Falling to pieces—those were your exact words."

Falling to pieces?

At that revelation, *two* indignant women glared at Sir Linnet.

He tugged at his collar. "I . . . well . . . I thought she seemed very angry—"

"Angry?" Aunt Honore's voice rose an octave. "Well, of course she was angry. Why wouldn't she be? If he'd said those things to me, I'd have shot the blighter. Had I known *angry* was the sentiment of the day, I'd have worn a red dress. Anger calls for something with flair. Something spicy. Not these blasted widow's tweeds."

"Honore! I'll thank you not to curse in my house. There are tender ears about." He gestured to the other girls who were creeping down the stairs, no doubt curious as to the cause of all the shouting.

"I didn't curse."

"*Blasted* is a—"

"Phfft! I can see you're as stuffy as ever. Why is it that all my brothers turned out to be so starchy? Our father would roll over in his grave."

Papa groaned. "Our father was a tyrant. Not half as tolerant as you always insist. You only think so because he doted on you. The rest of us—"

"Stop! I'll not hear another word against him." She glanced at the simple furnishings in the room. You've done tolerable well for yourself. Not bad for a third son. At least, I'm not bumping my head on the ceiling as I did at your nephew's hovel. Jerome is a vicar, did you know?" Before Papa could answer, she rattled on. "And a perfect bore. Never thought one of us could turn out so infernally dull. Father would take a stick—"

She stopped and pursed her lips at her brother. "Oh, never mind." Her attention darted away from Sir Linnet and landed with a hard squint on Kate's sisters. "Stop skulking on the stairs you three and come down here where you can be properly introduced."

Nora, Sadie, and Tilly scurried obediently into the parlor and lined up for inspection like charges before a governess. Honore snapped at her brother. "Well, don't stand there like a great lump. Introduce me."

He exhaled loudly. "You've met them before. Last summer to be exact, at Valen's wedding."

"That was ages ago. You can't expect me to remember all the way back to last summer. Who is this one?" She pinched Nora's cheek. "Pretty enough, I suppose, if you like the angelic sort. But far too pale. You read too much, my dear."

"This is Nora, and she is not pale." Papa put his arm around Nora's shoulders.

"Nora?!" Lady Alameda completely ignored his scold. "Dear, sweet Cavendish, did you name her after me? Oh, dearest brother, had I known—"

He rolled his eyes heavenward. "Nay, Honore. The child's proper name is Nora."

"*Nora?* Not Lenora or Honore?" Her nose scrunched up as if she smelled a rotting fish. "What kind of name is that? And she's still too pale."

Before he could find the words to respond, she moved on to Sadie. Lady Alameda circled, looking down her nose at the girl, appraising her with all the tact of a horse trader. When she grasped Sadie's chin, Kate half expected her to inspect the condition of her sister's teeth. Instead, the lady stepped back and uttered a satisfied grunt. "This one has promise. This is the one you ought to have named after me. Oh, yes. Look at the mischief in her eyes. Fire and spit. I like this one." She let go of Sadie's chin. "A pity about the red hair though. Perhaps we can do something about that."

Sadie took exception to this criticism. "It's not red, my lady. It is auburn."

Aunt Honore's brows lifted skeptically. "Call it what you will, my girl. Red is *très gauche.* Out of step. It needs to be remedied."

Tilly stepped forward in Sadie's defense. "You cannot improve upon God's handiwork."

"Is that a dare?" Lady Alameda frowned at Kate's youngest sister.

"No, my lady. It is merely a fact." Stouthearted little Tilly stood her ground, despite Countess de Alameda's imperious demeanor.

They stared at one another for a tense, overlong minute. Papa cleared his throat and was just on the verge of intervening when Lady Alameda spoke her mind. "You're trouble, aren't you?"

To which Tilly merely lifted one of her eyebrows.

"Humph. Obviously, you are, but at least you've got backbone. I'll give you that much. Whatever possessed you to speak out of turn? Haven't you ever been told that children should be seldom seen and *never* heard? How old are you, anyway? All of eight years?"

That miffed Tilly. "Ten!"

"Ha! Oh, well then. As ancient as that." Aunt Honore grinned. "Cavendish, I take back what I said about the other girl. What's her name? The redhead."

"Sadie." Tilly answered before her father could.

"Yes, Sadie. That fits." She dismissed their middle sister with a flick of her wrist and bore all her attention on Tilly. "It's not her who ought to be named after me. It's you. You're the one."

Tilly, the little rascal, curtsied elegantly enough to please a queen. "Matilda Honore Linnet, at your service, my lady."

"Ah-ha. I was right. My namesake. Perfect." Honore clapped her hands. "I shall mold you in my image."

"You'll do no such thing." Her father groaned.

Kate exchanged anxious glances with Nora. Tilly's middle name was not *Honore*.

"Everyone calls me Tilly." She grinned several shades too innocently at Honore's delight and her family's consternation, and Kate began to wonder if she might have underestimated her youngest sister.

The maid, Agnes, broke through Kate's stunned silence. She

hesitated in the parlor doorway and in a shy voice said to Kate, "Dinner is ready, miss."

Relieved to have a diversion from Tilly's tomfoolery, Kate gestured toward the dining room, "Shall we?"

Papa offered his arm to Lady Alameda and led her to the seat of honor at their humble table.

Throughout the meal, Kate felt as if the sword of Damocles hung above her head. She expected her sisters to spring their trap at any moment. Except they didn't. They remained on their best behavior.

Their *very* best behavior.

Quite unnerving.

No soup spilt. No peas flung across the table. All three girls ate with the dignity befitting a squire's table. They were perfect angels. And the more perfectly they behaved, the more polite they were to their guest, the more convinced Kate became that they had something sinister planned. A live frog in the baked pears. Poison in Aunt Honore's wine. Maybe they planned to drug the coachman. They were concocting some scheme to foil Kate's trip to London. Of that, she was certain.

The darling little conspirators respectfully asked Aunt Honore questions about London. What events did their aunt plan to attend? They begged her to tell them about the famous personages she knew. Had she supped at Carleton House with the Prince Regent? Oh, yes, she had, and Aunt Honore was more than happy to regale them with stories of how the rich and famous spent their evenings. Some of her stories were less than suitable for their young ears. Her father kept clearing his throat and giving his sister pointed glares.

Kate paid little heed to her aunt's tales. She was on high alert for worse things than the shocking behavior of some members of the *beau monde*. She kept a watchful eye out for tacks hidden in the chicken curry, or glue on her aunt's spoon. She had to be ready for anything.

When everyone except Kate laughed at Honore's anecdote, her aunt turned to her with a vexed frown. "You're awfully quiet. Are you ill? Or are you always this subdued?" She said *subdued* as if it were contagious, like the pox.

Sadie burst out laughing at that. "*Subdued?* Our Kate? You must not have heard about her dreadful temp—"

"Hush, Sadie." Nora glared, and Sadie promptly clamped her lips shut.

Kate responded to her aunt's inquiry. "I'm sorry if I seem overly quiet, my lady. I am merely eager to be on our way to London. I've never been. Your descriptions are so vivid. I'm all agog."

"Hhmm. *Agog?* Are you really? I wonder." Honore tapped the side of her wine glass with her fingernail. "You don't seem very gog-ish to me."

Tilly's nose turned up. "What does gog-ish mean? I've never heard—" Kate kicked her little sister underneath the table.

Chapter 3
Swift Falls the Sword

T ILLY RUBBED her abused shin and cast an injured grimace at
Kate until something outside the dining room window drew
the child's attention. Kate assumed it must be a butterfly or
a blue jay or some other innocuous creature, and merely felt
grateful that whatever fluttered by had distracted Tilly from crit-
icizing their aunt's faulty grammar.

In retrospect, Kate ought to have turned and checked.
Unfortunately, she faced away from the window, and it would've
been rude to crane her neck around like a goose to see what her
sister found so intriguing.

It wasn't until the knocker banged that Kate felt Damocles'
sword thump her rudely on the head. She overheard Agnes open
the door and say, "Afternoon, m'lord. I'm afraid the squire and all
the young ladies is sitting down to eat."

"That's all right. They're expecting me." A painfully familiar voice accosted Kate's ears. "I'll show myself in." His boots clicked against the floorboards.

Why didn't I look out the ruddy window?

I could've fled upstairs.

Kate winced and fought a mad urge to dive under the table.

Lord Colter.

Greyson.

She drew in a sharp breath and clutched the edge of the table. The wretched sword seemed to stab straight down through her stomach.

Agnes dutifully trailed behind Lord Colter. "Shall I set another place then, m'lord?"

"No need."

No need, indeed.

Lord Colter strode into the dining room, all annoying six feet of him.

"Good afternoon, ladies. Sir Linnet." He bowed graciously, and skimmed their faces until he landed on hers and grimaced. Kate didn't know if his dire expression was a reaction to the horror that must surely be written on her own features, or if it merely reflected his discomfiture at seeing her again.

Her father scraped back his chair and stood, surprise rendering him as speechless as Kate felt. Her throat tightened with unspoken words. She still held a white-knuckled grip on her table knife and briefly considered letting it do all the talking for her.

Father was at a complete loss for words. "Uh . . . Lord Colter . . . we hadn't expected to see you. That is to say—"

Kate found her tongue. "What in blazes are you doing here?"

"Kate!" her father scolded.

"I . . . that is to say . . ." Lord Colter glanced uncertainly at Sadie and Tilly before continuing. Tilly encouraged him with a broad smile, and Sadie nodded as if to say, *Get on with it.* He straightened to his full overbearing height. "I came to apologize."

"*What?*"

"Apologize."

That stumped Kate. She hadn't expected it from him. Devil take his boyishly disarming curls! She didn't give a fig about his roguishly dark eyes or his impossibly sun-kissed cheeks—though they were smooth-shaven for once, it was too little, too late.

"You consider that . . . that morsel, an apology?!" she sputtered. "A fat lot of good an apology will do now! *Here.* With only my family to hear it."

"Katherine!" her father cautioned, but she wasn't done.

"As far as the rest of the village is concerned, you've painted my character in the worst possible light. A *shrew.*" She practically spat it at him. "You may as well have tossed me onto the dung heap. You left me no future except that of an old maid!" The knife quivered in her fist.

Her skin blazed like the fires of hell.

She must surely be turning a bright shade of red, but oh, it felt good to hand him a piece of her mind. So good that she let her tongue dance forward, in one of those Spanish stomping dances. "If you were half a gentleman, you would take out a notice in the village newspaper. Although, now that I think on it, even that would be a useless gesture. It's doubtful an apology in print would repair my good name. People might think I'd henpecked you into writing it. No, sirrah, it is too late. I do not accept your apology. *Such as it is*, it's of no use to me at all."

His too-handsome face narrowed into a storm. "Of course not! Nothing I do is ever good enough for you, is it?" The heat in his words made her blood boil and the knife in her hand raised of its own accord. How dare he act as if *he* were the one wronged.

Oh, but he did dare, and he said more. "I came here, on bended knee, to tell you I'm sorry. And what do you do? You scrape me up one side and down the other with that wicked tongue of yours."

"Oh my." Aunt Honore tittered. "Such a *naughty* young man. I rather think you might enjoy a scraping of that sort."

"Honore!" Papa frowned at his sister. "I warned you about tender ears."

His scold only made things worse. Greyson's cheeks flushed scarlet. "That's not what I meant. I meant—"

"Everyone knows what you meant." Kate relished his embarrassment, but would rather he didn't repeat his thoughts about her character. "Even now, your opinion of me is quite clear. You would rather rot in hell than suffer ten more minutes in my company. That's what you said at the ball, and obviously it is still your attitude."

"Don't throw my words back at me."

She shook the knife at him, not on purpose, but merely because it was handy. "I can think of other things I'd prefer to throw."

He didn't look scared at all. "Put down the knife, Kate. We both know you wouldn't really use it on me."

"Oh, wouldn't I?" She hefted it, testing the weight in her palm. He was right, of course, but she wanted him to worry just a smidge.

"Throw it." This sage advice came from Aunt Honore. "Don't let him talk to you like that. You're no weakling. Give him a good jousting."

Honore's bloodthirsty taunts made Kate's anger tuck back into the dark pit of her stomach. Her aunt sounded like the Romans in the Colosseum must've when they shouted for gladiators to kill their opponents.

Kate took a deep breath and calmly set the knife down. "Why are you here, my lord? Clearly, it is not to apologize. For that must surely be the most pathetic attempt I have ever witnessed."

"Hardly an apology at all." Aunt Honore seemed annoyed that there would be no blood spilt. "And I never saw this *bended knee* he mentioned. Did you? Poorly done, young man. There was no heart in it."

"He meant it!" Sadie blurted, then drew back and meekly added, "I'm certain he did."

Tilly sat forward, nodding. "He does. This was all his idea."

Lord Colter glanced appreciatively at his supporters.

"His idea, *indeed.*" Kate leaned both hands on the table and glared past the bony partridge carcasses at all three of her sisters. "*They* put you up to this, didn't they?"

Sadie and Tilly squirmed. Nora flushed and looked away.

Greyson's features cooled, and he took a step in her direction, his hand out. "They merely came to me with their concerns, and I fully concur. You cannot go to London with Lady de Alameda. Her reputation precedes her. Begging your pardon, my lady. I mean no offense." He turned an earnest face to Aunt Honore, far more sincere than the half-baked apology he'd offered Kate.

Aunt Honore sniffed as if mildly intrigued. "I'm surprised you even know who I am."

"Everyone who's *anyone* knows who you are, Lady Alameda."

That seemed to gratify her somewhat. She surveyed him with a lorgnette that hung around her neck. "And you are?"

"Lord Colter, at your service." Greyson inclined his head.

"Are you?" Smiling like a sly barn cat, she held out her hand for him to pay homage.

When he straightened, he disappointed her by continuing his lecture on propriety. "Surely you realize, my lady, the circles you run in are not exactly suitable for an innocent such as Miss Linnet?"

"Are you saying the Prince Regent, ruler of our fair island and half the world, is not suitable company for my niece? I should think saying so borders on treason, young man."

"I . . . no! That's not what I meant."

"I should hope not. It would be a pity to watch you hang. Such a fine neck." Honore laughed coyly.

"Enough!" Kate stamped her slippered foot and crossed her arms. "I shall decide what circles are suitable for me and who ought to hang for it."

Lord *I-Know-Everything* Colter turned back to Kate. "Oh, do be sensible, Katherine. This is London we are talking about, and you know nothing of that world."

Aunt Honore guffawed at that. "And, you are so worldly-wise, because of being all of *what*; twenty years of age?"

"I am *four* and twenty, my lady. Only one year away from my majority, and more importantly, I have been to London."

"Four and twenty, you say? Oh dear me! So old. You're

practically in your dotage. I daresay you must know *everything* there is to know about London."

Greyson straightened and pushed up on his toes, as if adding an inch more to his six feet would make him wiser. "Mock me if you will. But I am sensible enough to know that Miss Linnet ought to stay here, in Clapsforth, where she can be kept safe."

"*Safe.*" Lady Alameda chuckled to herself as if he'd said something mildly humorous. She turned to Kate. "In my opinion, safety is vastly overrated. Is that what you want, my darling? To be *safe* and snug in this little village for the rest of your days?"

Kate's lips parted as she hunted for the answer.

What did she want?

Safety wasn't it, but neither did she want to endanger her future. Greyson stared at her, awaiting her response. Her sisters stared, too, and even her father. They were all leaving the decision to her.

It struck her then, with more force than the sword of Damocles, that she'd rarely had the freedom to choose anything in her life. In point of fact, she hadn't actually chosen Lord Colter. He'd chosen her. She certainly hadn't *chosen* to raise her younger sisters, or to keep house for her father. Apart from what dress she would slip over her head in the morning, what had she ever chosen for herself?

Nothing.

Not one thing.

Aunt Honore sliced into Kate's thoughts. "Kate, dear, I'll admit this young man is fairly pleasant on the eyes, and . . . well . . . rather appealing in a rustic fashion." The woman smiled flirtatiously at Lord Colter.

No, *not flirtatiously.*

Her expression was downright seductive. Luckily, Greyson wasn't looking at Kate's devilish aunt. Failing to draw his attention, Honore shrugged and continued lecturing Kate. "You mustn't let him tempt you. You must come to London. I insist upon it. You're to be my protégé, and there's an end to the matter."

"Your protégé?" What did her aunt mean? Kate intended this to be a visit to London for the remainder of the season. Nothing more.

"What's a protégé?" Tilly demanded.

"It's a French word," Aunt Honore said.

Tilly pinched up her little nose. "Yes, but what does it mean?"

Honore's nose pinched up in almost the same manner. "Oh, fiddlesticks. You and your definitions. It means something like a *project.*"

Tilly nodded, pretending to be far more wizened than she was. "I see. A project—like when Papa said that we all had to pitch in and help build a new pig pen? That sort of project?"

"Precisely." Honore flicked her hand shooing Tilly away. Then she harumphed rather loudly. "You are weakening, Katherine Linnet. I see it in your eyes."

Kate wasn't weakening, but she didn't like the idea of being her aunt's latest project, either. Perhaps she ought to stay put. Lord Colter had a point. She knew nothing of London.

"No, don't look at him like that," Honore snapped. "Do try and remember it was he who publicly jilted you last Thursday.

Her aunt's words hit the mark. The woman may as well have

catapulted a boulder at Kate. That horrid night flashed through her mind again.

How numb she'd felt after his public castigation. She would never forget how the blood seemed to drain from her head, leaving her faint, despite the fires of humiliation scorching her chest. It had taken every ounce of her strength not to collapse under the realization that her life had just ended. Instead, she had turned, white-faced, and walked silently out of the assembly rooms, staring straight ahead into the blackness of the night and her future.

Kate dropped into her chair with a thud, only able to nod.

"None of that matters." Greyson rushed to her side. "Be sensible, Kate. Think of your sisters. You can't go haring off to London—"

Her sisters.

Sensible Kate had been watching over them for the last ten years. She was tired of thinking of her sisters. Tired of being sensible. "Why do you care? You broke our engagement and you said—"

"Words spoken in haste." He pressed his lips together before continuing, but then he barged straight forward into the truth. If only he would leave the truth out of it. "Thing is, Kate, you *were* needling me at every turn. *Do this. Don't do that. Go ask poor old Miss Blumsbury to dance. Must you drink so much champagne? Stand up straighter. Don't laugh so loudly.*" He stopped recounting his grievances and lowered his head for a moment. When he looked up again, melancholy darkened the brown of his eyes. "All that badgering wears on a man."

Summed up like that, she felt shame worming into her

resolve.

She was a shrew.

He hadn't said any of it accusatorially. He didn't even sound angry. She felt grateful for that. It could've been worse. He didn't even mention any of her other disparaging remarks. After all, she had teased him about his dancing skills, and jested about the way his Adam's apple bobbled up and down as it squeezed over his too-tight collar. And a bushel of other things.

Kate studied him for a moment. He still smelled faintly of his shaving soap, fresh and clean, and yet in places his beard hairs were already peeking through his cheeks and chin. She smiled at the way his hair fell in careless waves through no artifice on his part. She was jealous of his long eyelashes and the warm brown of his eyes, although she didn't envy the permanent lump on his nose. She remembered the day he'd fallen out of a tree and broken it. He'd been no older than Tilly.

Greyson was a good friend, maybe one of her closest. Why then had she kept badgering him with petty grievances ever since they'd gotten engaged?

Then it hit her squarely between the eyes . . . the real reason. *Well*, she certainly had no intention of confessing that to him or anyone else.

"You're right." Kate bowed her head. "I *was* needling you. And for that I am truly sorry." She also understood exactly why she'd been needling him. For the first time in what seemed like a hundred years, Kate had a moment of perfect clarity.

She knew exactly what she wanted.

Freedom.

Freedom to do *what*, she had no earthly idea, but she knew

she'd never find it here in Clapsforth. She turned to her aunt. "If you are still willing to have me, I would very much like to come to London with you."

"No!" Greyson stood. His words shot out with too much force. "No. You can't go. I forbid it, Katherine."

She smiled serenely at him. "I believe you'll find, my lord, that I can. You surrendered the right to forbid me *anything* when you broke off our engagement."

"I take it all back." He dropped down on one knee. "Don't go, Kate. Stay. Marry me!"

Kate liked him better in that moment than she had in her entire life. In fact, she realized she might actually love him. Sadly, not enough. She gently cupped his cheek and shook her head. "I'm sorry. Now, if you will excuse me, I must go and change into my traveling clothes."

She stood and felt genuine sorrow when Greyson dropped his head into his hands and sagged over his knee.

Aunt Honore smiled wickedly.

Chapter 4
The Trouble with Sisters

K ATE ALMOST ESCAPED the dining room.

"Wait." Nora's voice stopped her. If it had been anyone else, she would have kept walking. "Please, Kate. I would like to come with you."

There was something painfully earnest in Nora's plea. The girl so rarely asserted herself that it took Kate completely by surprise. The look on her sister's face tore Kate's resolve to shreds.

Nora was beautiful in a way that would've enthralled great painters. She had an otherworldly quality that went far beyond angelic, yet she seemed completely unaware of her beauty. Men young and old sighed when Nora passed by and their eyes softened with indulgent expressions that would've made the queen envious. On those rare occasions when Nora drew upon her transcendent appeal, there was little anyone could deny her.

And Kate knew it.

"Please?" Nora asked again, with a kindness that pierced Kate's flinty heart. Seeing she'd won Kate's silent consent; Nora turned to Aunt Honore and gently redirected her request. "May I accompany my sister? I will happily sleep at the foot of her bed, and I promise I shall not be any trouble."

Aunt Honore's lips parted in astonishment. She stared at Nora as if she had never seen the girl before. She probably hadn't—not really. Kate was a little surprised to see that even the cynical countess was not immune to her sister's uncanny allure.

"Dear heavens, I had no idea you were so . . ." Aunt Honore blinked and struggled to find words. "You *aren't* pale." She looked away and seemed to regain some of the customary hardness in her own features. "Very well. Yes, you may come."

Honore still seemed half mesmerized as she reached for her wine glass. "Although I suspect you will be a *great deal* of trouble. Bound to leave a trail of broken hearts all across Mayfair." She tossed back a fortifying gulp of wine.

Sadie jumped to her feet. "Me too! I want to come. I'll sleep on the floor, too."

"Good gracious, child. Don't be ridiculous. No one sleeps on the floor at my house, not even the scullery maid."

"Excellent!" Sadie grinned. "I shall be happy to sleep in a bed."

Aunt Honore sputtered. "Wait. What? That's not what I—"

"We should all go." Tilly stood and grabbed Sadie's hand. She dimpled up at Aunt Honore. "You wouldn't want to leave your namesake behind, would you?"

Honore's mouth fell open. "*All* of you?"

"Girls!" Papa smacked the table, rattling the silverware. "Stop begging favors of Lady Alameda. Anyone would think you were raised in Spitalfields." He glared at Sadie and Tilly. "What can you be thinking, behaving like this? Placing demands upon your aunt. Anyone can see she is not up to the task of watching over *all* of you. That would be asking far too much for a woman of her age—"

"A woman of my *what*?" Honore squawked, setting her glass down with a plunk.

"But Papa, I wasn't begging." Tilly stuck out her chin. "I was merely stating a fact." She edged closer to Sadie. "Wheresoever my sisters goeth, there shall I go also."

Honore looked aghast at her brother. "What is it with your youngest and her obsession with biblical edicts and annoying *facts*?" She whipped back to Tilly. "If you're going to be quoting scripture, my girl, you can no longer be my namesake."

Tilly primly tilted her head to her aunt. "I assure you, my lady, it wasn't scripture."

Not scripture, *exactly*, but close enough. Kate narrowed her gaze at her baby sister. The child's prevarications were beginning to stack up at an alarming rate.

Honore sniffed skeptically. "I distinctly heard you say the word 'goeth,' and that sounds awfully biblical to me."

"I was merely paraphrasing a young lady named Ruth."

"Oh, well, that's all right then." Lady Alameda forgave Tilly and turned her ire back on Papa. "Listen here, brother dear, I am decades younger than you. *Centuries* younger! How dare you call me a woman of my age?"

At this juncture, Lord Colter helped himself to Kate's

vacated chair. As he watched matters unfolding like a bad play, his countenance wavered between confusion and astonishment. He also helped himself to the remainder of Kate's wine, slugging it back like brandy, and promptly refilling the glass.

"You know perfectly well you are only five years my junior." Kate's father wearily corrected his sister. "And yes, I dared call you a woman of your age because you *are* a woman of your age. What other age can you possibly be?"

"Any age I wish!"

"I see. You rule over *time* now, do you?" He let out an exasperated huff. "Don't spout nonsense. Aside from that, you're missing the point, Honore. It would be too much for you to care for all four of my daughters. You couldn't possibly manage it."

"Why not?" she snapped. "*You* see to their care. And I'm not nearly as decrepit an old goat as *you* are." She pursed her lips indignantly.

Papa wasn't an old goat. That was unfair. Kate noticed Tilly about to dive in and defend their father. Luckily, Sadie noticed too and delivered a sharp nudge and quick shake of her head, warning Tilly not to interfere.

Sadie wasn't trying to keep Tilly from being rude. A slow half-smile curled impishly on her cheek. She must've noticed that the more Papa fought to stop them from going, the more Aunt Honore insisted they should.

She was right. Papa's well-meaning arguments were turning the tide as surely as the moon. Kate sighed, feeling her tiny hope of freedom ebbing out to sea.

"For your information," Papa blustered, "I'm in fine fettle—hale and hearty." He all but beat against his chest to prove it.

"Look at you, Honore. You're skin and bone. You stay out gaming and dancing your way across London until the cock crows. You drink too much, and you're not used to tending to anyone's needs except your own. Unless I miss my guess your most bothersome task is visiting the dressmaker and standing still for a fitting."

Honore rolled her eyes. "Don't be silly. I don't stand around for fittings. They have my measurements on file."

"There! You see, you've made my point. It's no stroll in the park looking after four daughters. It requires self-sacrifice and . . . and watchfulness. You've no idea the burdens you would be taking on. There's endless squabbles and . . ."

Kate stared at her father, unaware he felt that she and her sisters were such a heavy burden. How could that be, when she had been the one doing all the work?

He continued elaborating on what an onerous task it was to look after them and ended rather bluntly. "You can't do it, Honore. You can't! You've no experience, and you don't have the strength of character it requires."

Honore's chin shot up the same way Tilly's does when she's in a stubborn mood. "You're wrong, brother dear. I raised my stepson, Marcus. Not only that, I've had the care and keeping of *several* nieces."

"Two nieces." He thrust out two fingers, but tucked his hand away when his sister swatted at it. "And those were very well-behaved young ladies, not like this band of scamps."

Scamps?

Is that what he thinks of us?

Aunt Honore waved his criticism away with a haughty sniff. "You're forgetting Fiona. The *beau monde* dubbed her Lady Fiasco.

The girl caused a mishap at nearly every gathering. If I can handle her—"

"*You didn't.* That's the rub. Everyone knows what happened to her on your watch."

"Oh, pooh!" Lady Alameda sat back and crossed her arms. "It all landed sunny-side up, didn't it? She married well and has two brats of her own, last I heard."

"No thanks to you."

Honore glared something fierce at Papa, and Kate wondered if any minute her aunt's nostrils might start spewing steam. "You *impervious* old buzzard! You have no idea what I did, or didn't do, for that girl."

"You mean imperious, don't you?" Tilly had been reading too much of Samuel Johnson's dictionary.

"Same thing," Aunt Honore snapped.

"Not really—" Tilly got a hard elbow to the ribs from Sadie.

Papa crossed his arms looking every bit as stubborn as his fire-breathing sister. "I won't allow them to go."

"You most certainly will! You wrote to me. *Remember?* Begging me to come to your aid. Here I am, rendering assistance."

"I asked for your help with Kate. Only Kate. Not the whole passel of them."

"*Passel.* Tch, tch." She wagged her finger at him. "And you have the gall to scold me for my language. That's not a very affectionate term, Cavendish. Mind your manners."

"Passel means—"

Papa's hand lifted to stop Tilly's explanation. Then he dropped it to the table. The fight went out of him. "What's the use? It's not my intention to argue with you, Honore. I'd lose anyway. It was always that way between us, wasn't it?"

She sniffed, and the barbs in her tone vanished. "Think of it like this: I shall be sparing you the cost of at least three London come-outs."

Kate watched her father sit back and calculate in his head the cost of taking his daughters to London for the season. Plus, it would be more than one season if any of them failed to secure husbands on the first go. The expenses for housing and gowns would be enormous, which went a long way toward explaining why he'd invited Lady Alameda to help Kate in the first place. Since her engagement to Lord Colter had gone up in a blazing puff of smoke, Papa was trying to give her a way to find happiness.

Aunt Honore knew Papa better than Kate had guessed. Bringing up the expense of a London season was a brilliant ploy. His sister knew precisely where to stab the needle and tie the knot in her argument. "Surely you don't expect all four of your daughters to marry backwater boys like this one?" She gestured at Lord Colter.

Lord Colter raised his head from his third glass of wine. "I am not a backwater boy. I'll have you know I went to Eton and Cambridge."

"Did you?" She lifted her lorgnette and surveyed him, one eyebrow lifting appreciatively. "Interesting." Her mouth twitched curiously before dismissing him with a wave of her jewel-encrusted fingers and turning back to Kate's sisters. "Do you girls wish to come with me to London or not?"

Sadie and Tilly nodded like eager woodenheaded puppets. Nora edged closer to Kate, looking more and more uncertain about the way events were unfolding.

"Splendid." Honore clapped her hands together. "Go on, then. Pack your things." She shooed them away. "*Quickly.* I intend to leave in half an hour."

Sadie and Tilly tore out of the room. Nora trailed after them. Kate leaned against the doorframe. Well, that was that. She wouldn't be free after all. There could be no doubt as to who would actually be looking after her sisters, and it certainly wouldn't be her aunt. She emitted a low moan.

Papa shook his head and pressed his hands flat against the table. "No good can come of this, Honore. You're doing what you always do—behaving like a petulant child."

Honore rose and shook the crumbs out of her black silk skirts. "Thank you, Cavendish. You always know the exact right things to say."

"I don't see how you can manage this. You don't have a motherly bone in your body." He sounded genuinely worried.

"Perhaps not." She smiled unabashedly. "But you'll be pleased to hear I have several *aunt-ly* bones."

"*Aunt-ly*?" He sighed. "There's no such thing, and you know it. You'll be hauling the girls back before the week is out."

"We'll see about that, shall we?" His sister kissed the top of his graying head.

"Do a favor for me, will you?" He caught her hand and asked earnestly, "At least bring them back alive."

To that, she merely laughed, shook him loose, and strolled out of the room. "Now, where did my coachmen and footmen wander off to? The kitchens, I suppose."

Her father slumped in his chair. "This is a disaster."

"You won't get an argument from me." Lord Colter pushed

back from the table and strode to Katherine, pinning her in the doorway.

He stood too close.

So close she could almost taste the wine on his breath. He towered over her, staring down at her with the oddest expression. She wasn't sure if he intended to shake her or kiss her. *Or maybe both.* He leaned closer and she began to think he intended the latter. She hoped so. It would be exceedingly pleasant to kiss him farewell.

They'd kissed before. *Twice.*

The second time had been on the occasion of their engagement, a quick and furtive peck. The first time, however, had been . . .

Quite lovely.

She'd been only fifteen. Greyson had returned home from school for the winter holidays. There'd been a glorious snowfall the Saturday after Boxing Day, and half the village gathered on the hill north of the river to do a bit of sliding. Late in the day, after nearly everyone else had gone home, Kate took a bad tumble into the trees, and Greyson came running to her rescue, laughing when he found her buried in the snow. He pulled her out, retrieved her rickety old sled, and found her bonnet that had been torn off in the crash.

It happened when he stood brushing snow out of her hair and off her shoulders, and they'd realized they were all alone in the trees. His hands had slowed and drifted down her arms. She would never forget the eager way his mouth covered hers, almost as if he wanted to devour her. She often thought back on that day, wishing she'd known how to respond. Despite her inexperience, their first kiss had left her breathless and exhilarated. When he finally let go of her, they stared at one another in surprise. After that, she'd never looked at him the same way.

And now, as Greyson stared at her, drawing nearer and nearer, she softened her mouth, *hoping*. He clasped the sides of her face in his palms and she was sure he would kiss her.

Except he didn't.

He stared at her mouth as if he were angry at her lips. Or was he hungry for them? No, that was definitely anger. "This isn't over, Kate."

Chapter 5
Travel Travails

HE LEFT HER. Just like that, Lord Colter marched out of her father's house, and left her clutching the doorframe to keep her balance. No farewell kiss.

No farewell at all.

Devil take him. He was a nuisance anyway. Good riddance, she told herself. Except Kate couldn't drum up enough anger to carry herself forward with any energy. She stumbled upstairs and dropped wearily into a chair, ostensibly to oversee her sisters' packing. Except she didn't oversee it. Ralphie trotted up beside her and lay his head on her lap. She absentmindedly ruffled her fingers through his soft fur.

Nora nervously paced closer while folding a petticoat. "It's better that we're coming with you to London. This way we'll all be there together." She waited for Kate to respond. "To watch out for each other. Like we always do."

Like we always do?

That jolted Kate out of her daze. "I can take care of myself, thank you very much. And I absolutely refuse to play nursemaid to all of you. I'm done with that. This was supposed to be *my* trip to London. Not yours." She waved Nora away. "You three are on your own. See to yourselves. I'll not have you spoiling my last chance at happiness."

"Happiness?" Sadie looked up from rolling up a pair of stockings. "Surely you don't mean you are looking to find happiness on London's marriage mart? Landing a husband—that's what the season is for, you know. Not happiness. The season is a perilous undertaking. Marry the wrong man and—"

"Do not presume to educate me, *little* sister." Kate sniffed with considerable irritation at Sadie. "For your information, I do not wish to be a spinster for the rest of my life."

Sadie stuffed the stockings into her small portmanteau. "If that's what you're fretting about, why don't you stay here and marry Lord Colter?"

"Don't be ridiculous. I intend to find someone with whom I can be happy rather than miserable. More importantly, someone who lives far away from Clapsforth." Kate shooed Ralphie aside.

"Far away? Away from us?" Tilly planted herself directly in front of Kate, and with a pointed frown marring her perfect features, she stamped her foot.

Kate squirmed in her chair, not wanting to answer, but Tilly continued to spear her with a relentless accusatorial glare. So, Kate made something up. "I should like a household of my own. Would you deny me that?"

Tilly pursed her lips skeptically.

"Balderdash," muttered Sadie.

They were right. It was a terrible lie. The last thing Kate wanted was the responsibilities of a household. She couldn't very well tell them the truth—that she was starving for even a morsel of independence, that she was suffocating here in Clapsforth, and that taking care of them was turning her into an unmarriageable shrew. Marrying Lord Colter would simply layer on more burdens, and what if she had children? Heaven help her! Kate's stomach cinched up tighter than a hangman's noose.

In lieu of trying to defend herself, Kate decided to flee the room, but at the last minute, she turned in the doorway and laid out one more lie. "And anyway, none of you need me anymore. You'll be perfectly fine on your own."

Half an hour later, the footmen having strapped four trunks and a dozen hatboxes atop Aunt Honore's coach, Kate and her sisters bid their father adieu and climbed aboard. Aunt Honore dictated the seating. Kate, Nora, and Sadie squeezed onto the bench across from Honore and her namesake. Sadie pointed out that since Tilly was the smallest of the sisters, she ought to trade with one of them. Lady Alameda responded sharply, "Nonsense! I don't care to be cramped while traveling. Bad enough your father tricked me into bringing all of you to town—I refuse to be otherwise inconvenienced."

A harbinger of things to come, thought Kate.

Not only were they were squeezed in tighter than an old lady's corset, Honore assigned Kate, Sadie, and Nora the rear facing seat. An unfortunate situation for Kate, as she was prone to travel sickness, especially when facing backward.

They were only twenty minutes down the road when Kate began to blame her roiling stomach on nerves. Then she changed her mind and decided the curried lamb was responsible for her discomfort. No, wait. It was probably the rich cream sauce in the *Soupe à la Flamond*. Or perhaps the partridge had been under-done. Whatever the culprit, luncheon was threatening to make an encore appearance.

Aunt Honore made a low growling noise. "What's the matter with you? You look positively green."

Nora took one look at Kate and began rubbing Kate's back. "My sister gets travel-sick, especially when facing the wrong way."

"Well then, don't just sit there! Change places with her. Let her sit closer to the window. Lower the glass. Give her some air." Honore moved as far from Kate as possible and lowered the other window glass as well.

"Thank you," Kate managed to say, leaning toward the breeze coming in.

"If you plan on casting up your accounts, kindly do it out the window." Honore tucked her skirts closer. "Or into your reticule. I won't have you ruining my calfskin upholstery."

Kate's malady had little effect on Sadie. She took advantage of the lowered window on her side of the coach and leaned out to look around.

"Listen here, *Red*." Honore clucked her tongue at Sadie. "Unless you are sick too, I won't have you hanging your head out the window and dangling your tongue like an idiotic mongrel. This is not a mail coach, and you are not a country bumpkin."

Tilly spoke up for her sister. "Seeing as we are from the

country—"

"I take it back, Little Miss Dictionary." Honore frowned at Tilly and turned back to Sadie. "You may be country bumpkins, but I expect you to resist behaving as such."

"Perhaps you need glasses. I'm not dangling my tongue. Nor would I ever." Sadie frowned at their aunt as if Honore might be slightly daft. "But look." She leaned out the window again and pointed. "Someone is following us."

Lady Alameda pinched up her mouth and exhaled loudly. "Were you born yesterday? There are bound to be other travelers on the road, child. That is what roads are for. Now pull in your arm *this instant*! I swear, next time I take the lot of you in my coach, I will have my coat of arms covered up. You're an embarrassment."

Sadie seemed oblivious to the criticism. "It's coming fast! And I think it might be . . . *ohhh*." She sat back against the leather seats and nudged Nora. Nora leaned across her sister and then flopped back, glancing furtively at Kate.

But it was Tilly who barked, "What is it? What did you see?" She slid off the seat and leaned out of the window, straining to see. "Where? There's nothing there. I can't see anything except dust—"

Aunt Honore grabbed Tilly's sash and yanked her back onto the seat. "If you fall out of that window, I am not stopping this coach to go back and retrieve your carcass. Do you understand?"

Big-eyed, Tilly nodded at their fearsome aunt.

Kate glanced out of her window and saw exactly why Tilly couldn't see the other traveler. The approaching vehicle—a light, well-sprung curricle pulled by a matched set of bays—raced toward them. In order to pass Aunt Honore's coach, it had moved to the other side of the road.

"*Greyson*," she said under her breath. He slowed as he passed them and the scoundrel tipped his hat at her.

Tipped his hat. Playing the part of a flirtatious young buck. His parting words rattled through her head. *This isn't over.* Stubborn man. The rascal cast her a smug self-satisfied grin and raced his team past their lumbering coach.

Kate's agitated breaths galloped faster than his horses. She frantically tried to pull up the window glass. It wasn't lost on her that he had strapped a large traveling trunk to his tiger stand.

Honore leaned forward. "Looks as if your young man is going to London, too. Bravo! An intelligent move. I'm beginning to like this lad."

"He's not a lad. He's a reckless, obstinate . . ." Unable to pull up the glass, Kate yanked down the black shade. It flapped in the breeze. She slammed back against the seat with her arms crossed tight against her chest. "Problem."

Aunt Honore tilted her head. "I thought you were travelsick?"

"Oh, I am! I am."

Her aunt merely laughed.

Lord Colter and her sisters were ruining everything. Travelsick and peeved, Kate closed her eyes and tried to think. What could she do? She had precious few options, but she ran through them all the same.

She could beg Aunt Honore to turn around immediately, and take her back home where she would spend the rest of her life in Clapsforth, *miserable*.

Or they could travel on to London where her sisters and her ex-fiancé would undoubtedly sabotage her debut into society, thus making her equally *miserable*.

Or . . .

She could take matters into her own hand.

Right there, sitting in her aunt's coach with lunch bubbling up her throat like lava, Kate made a decision. Greyson and her sisters might be pigheaded enough to traipse after her to London, but she had more grit than they did. She wouldn't let them ruin this for her.

Not only that, Kate would prove they were wrong for not trusting her to make a success of it on her own. She would singlehandedly turn herself into the belle of the season. She would charm all of London and dance her way into the hearts of the *beau monde*. She, Miss Kate Linnet, would become the darling of the season, even if she had to do it with Greyson and her sisters clinging to her ankles.

Kate straightened and lifted her chin. She swallowed hard and snapped the roller shade back up, blinking into the sunshine with the cool-headed determination of a warrior queen. She would show him. And she would show those scurvy gossips back in Clapsforth. She would show them all!

"Hmm." Aunt Honore tilted her head studying Kate from the far corner of the coach. "When you stop brooding, you look a lot less like yesterday's porridge."

"Thank you, my lady. High praise indeed."

Aunt Honore tried to hide her smile, but Kate noticed.

Chapter 6
Perils of a Coffee Room

K ATE HAD A PLAN and her stomach felt immeasurably better for it. During the next few hours, she felt very little inclination to cascade on her aunt's soft-as-a-lamb's-bottom leather seats. Not until they clattered through the courtyard of a coaching inn did her queasiness return. Her stomach turned sour the moment she recognized Lord Colter's curricle. His vehicle sat unhitched on the side of the courtyard, sprawled there like the abandoned skeletal remains of some ghastly creature.

Kate groaned and pleaded, "Can we not stop elsewhere?"

"There is no *elsewhere*," her aunt retorted. "We are in the middle of nowhere."

The ostler's horn, announcing their arrival, blew louder than Gabriel's trump.

Tilly woke up with a start. "Are we in London?"

"Heavens no, child." Aunt Honore looked down her nose at her would-be namesake. "We are only halfway. This is the Bell and Horn, a coaching house. My horses need refreshing and so do I." Her footman opened her door and lowered the steps.

Like chicks following a hen, they traipsed after their aunt into the establishment. The air inside the coaching house hung thick with the fragrance of too many travelers. The smell of sweat mingled with roasted chicken, tobacco smoke, ale, and over-steeped tea. Laughter and boisterous chatter overshadowed the host's greeting. All the windows were open, yet the place felt dim for want of light. The innkeeper ushered them forward until they stood in front of a desk. "Apologies, m'lady. We've only two private parlors, and both of them are taken up. But we've plenty o' tables in the common rooms." He gestured as if welcoming us to enter and squeeze into the crowded room.

"Reeaally?" Aunt Honore's disapproving tone brought a blush to the proprietor's cheeks. "Only two parlors."

He fussed with his drooping neckcloth and drew her attention to his logbook. "I'm very sorry, m'lady, but we've had a rash of travelers. 'Tis that time of the year, you see?" True enough, the ostler's horn kept blowing and a line of patrons was forming behind them.

"And rooms?" She spoke loud enough to be heard over a burst of laughter from the main hall. "I trust you have suitable accommodations for my nieces and myself."

His smile wobbled uncertainly. "Uh, yes. That is to say, we do if the young ladies here are willing to share a room amongst themselves."

"Share?" Lady Alameda reared up as if he'd suggested they

all bed down in the stables.

"I've a chamber with a rather large bed, yer ladyship. It should accommodate them well enough. And there's a tidy room right next to theirs for yourself." He tried to hand her the quill to sign his book. When she made no move to take it, he cleared his throat. "As you've been somewhat inconvenienced, I shall mark a shilling off the cost of both rooms. Will that suit ye?"

"Only one?" Her brow twitched. "Mark off two shillings, and I might be persuaded to make do with these inferior accommodations."

While Lady Alameda negotiated with the innkeeper, Kate peered into the musty depths of the Bell and Horn. Greyson was here, somewhere amidst the crowded tangle of humanity. She could practically feel him breathing down her neck. At the thought, she turned suddenly, thinking he might truly be standing behind her, but it was only Nora. And behind her, a tall, young gentleman in a smart, triple-caped greatcoat and a handsomely tailored jacket of bottle green underneath. She was staring, she realized, and he at her. She turned away, but Tilly was also staring. "Excuse me, sir, but aren't you hot in that big coat?"

He doffed his top hat to little Tilly, revealing a head full of divine curls. With a pleasant glint in his expression, he smiled and answered, "I am, indeed. However, I had to wear it because I've been riding atop my carriage to better take in the scenery, and one never knows when it might rain, does one?"

Tilly, ever the serious widgeon, found this a suitable response and nodded. "True. This is England, after all." She was parroting Father, and sounded more like an ancient busybody than a ten-year-old. "You're wise, sir, to be prepared. I am Matilda

Linnet. Pleased to make your acquaintance."

"My apologies, sir." Nora tried to tug Tilly away. "Tilly dearest, one mustn't introduce oneself. It simply isn't done."

"Fiddle-dee-dee." Tilly stood her ground. "We're still in the country and seeing as we are all to be jammed together in the coffee room, what can be the harm in it?"

The young man bowed graciously. "The pleasure is all mine, Miss Linnet." He smiled at all four of them. "Lord Weatherford, at your service. Now that we have introduced ourselves, young lady, perhaps you would do me the honor of introducing me to your lovely sisters."

Lady Alameda finished rubbing the innkeeper's nose in his inadequacies, and spun around to see who was accosting her nieces. Her eyes opened wide, her lashes fluttered, and she transformed from outraged matron to simpering flirt inside of one tick of the clock. "La! As I live and breathe, if it isn't Lord Weatherford! What a pleasant surprise to run into you here—of all places. In such a . . ." She touched a gloved finger to the paneled wall as if it were smeared with years of grease and dust instead of well-worn and polished. "Rustic setting."

He bowed graciously. "Been visiting friends. Did a bit of fishing on the river."

"And how is your father?"

"Not well, I'm afraid. Heart trouble."

"Not apoplexy, surely? He seemed in fine fettle when I saw him last."

"Not pain of that sort, my lady. I'm afraid he has not recovered from the wound you dealt him."

"Don't be preposterous." She whipped out her fan and

created a breeze for her reddened cheeks. "There can be no wound where no blow was dealt. Your father and I are still friends."

He allowed the next guest in line to take his spot in front of the innkeeper. "I do not mean to scold. After all, a lady as extraordinarily beautiful as yourself cannot be held responsible for all the broken hearts left in her wake."

The heartbreaker's four charges studied their aunt with considerable interest. Honore's cheeks cooled and she fanned a little less vigorously. "Oh, pish-posh. Now you're flambé-ing me."

Tilly raised her finger in protest. "No, Auntie, a flambé is rum cake or pudding set on fire. You probably meant to say *flummery*, which is also a pudding, but sometimes refers to flattery. In either case, I don't believe you can use it as a verb."

"I just did!" Lady Alameda pressed her lips into a tight, irritated, *so-there* smile.

Kate made a mental note to burn Doctor Johnson's dictionary before her little sister read any more of it.

"*Auntie?*" Lord Weatherford drew back in mock surprise. "What! Don't tell me these angels are your nieces? I should've guessed. Such exquisite beauties could not possibly be related to anyone else." He doffed his hat again and grinned at them.

Aunt Honore did nothing to deny the compliment. Instead, she swept the lot of them back behind her. "Very prettily said, but do remember they are young and impressionable, not used to your flummery-ing." She cast a sneer over her shoulder at Tilly.

"I protest, my lady. T'was neither flummery nor flambé. I meant every word." He grinned and perused Nora and Kate appreciatively. "After I secure my lodgings, you must allow me to buy supper for all of you."

Aunt Honore tapped her chin with the tip of her fan. "I suppose there's no harm in that."

His eyes brightened as he stepped up and took his turn at the innkeeper's desk.

The girls followed their aunt to a table in the corner of the coffee room. Kate hoped her bonnet would hide her from Lord Colter, who might be lurking somewhere in the stuffy, overcrowded room.

It was a vain hope—a vain hope, indeed. Kate instantly spotted the rascal leaning against the far wall where he had a clear view of their entrance. She ducked and turned away, praying he hadn't noticed her. A futile precaution. She and her three sisters looked like a string of bright yellow ducklings following an extremely notable black swan. It would be impossible to miss them.

Everyone in the coffee room observed their entrance. Gentlemen jumped up offering their tables to Lady Alameda as if she were the Queen of England instead of an Englishwoman who'd had the good fortune to marry a wealthy Spanish count. She declined their offers and paddled across the busy pond, setting her sights on a table in the far corner. Its lone occupant vacated his seat hurriedly at her approach, bowing to Lady Alameda and stammering wordlessly.

Kate and her sisters didn't even have enough time to arrange themselves around the table when Lord Colter pushed off from the wall and headed straight for them. "Ladies." He bowed graciously, just as if he and Kate hadn't shared a frightfully upsetting disagreement six hours earlier. "How fortuitous to run into you here at the Bull and Horn."

"Fortuitous?" Kate drew in a sharp breath, calmed her irritation, and did her best to mimic her aunt's sophisticated tone. "Oh yes, quite the happenstance, considering this is the only coaching inn on this road until one reaches the outskirts of London."

Aunt Honore chuckled. "She's right, you know."

"No," he insisted tugging at his collar. "There *are* other choices." He straightened his vest and lost his charming smile. "The Singing Magpie is a mere fifteen miles farther, and only a short jaunt off the main road. Granted, it is more of a tavern, but a choice nonetheless."

"Why, Lord Colter, you surprise me." Honore touched her glove gingerly to the table, flicking a breadcrumb to the floor. "You do know how The Singing Magpie got its name, do you not?" She smiled slyly at him.

He rubbed his neck. "Well, er, I may have heard something, but I don't believe that's an appropriate topic for—"

"Is there a flock of magpies nearby?" Tilly leaned closer to their aunt. "And do they sing terribly loud and keep travelers awake?"

"Oh, yes. *Abominably* loud." Honore chuckled and checked the tips of her gloves for more crumbs. The sly way she kept laughing gave Kate the distinct impression that she referred to something far less innocent than noisy birds.

Aunt Honore warmed to her subject. "The clientele there are often heard—"

"You need not say anything more about it." Kate pressed a hand to her already roiling stomach. "We comprehend your meaning and shall happily avoid the place."

Greyson pressed closer. "Are you unwell, Katherine?"

"I am perfectly fine, thank you." She lied. Her head throbbed and her stomach felt as if a beastly flock of magpies were trapped inside.

Lord Colter leaned solicitously over her. "I took the liberty of reserving one of the private parlors. You may all join me in—"

"No, thank you." Kate backed away and spoke so sharply that a family seated nearby turned to stare in their direction. She lowered her voice. "We shall do perfectly well out here."

"Don't be stubborn, Kate. I'm offering you a private parlor. A courtesy to a friend, nothing more."

Friend? A courtesy? Kate set her jaw. They wouldn't be here at all if he had been courteous to her at the assembly ball.

"Very *kind* of you, I'm sure." She hoped he noted the sarcasm dripping from each word. "But we are infinitely more comfortable where we are. Thank you, my lord."

Greyson gritted his teeth and turned to Lady Alameda. "My lady, surely you and your young charges would enjoy the benefit of a private parlor?"

"Oh, no." Aunt Honore's brows tilted upward and a smirk colored her answer. "At the moment, I'm rather enjoying the entertainment out here."

Nora, ever the voice of reason, no matter how irritating that might be to Kate, cleared her throat. "Katie, perhaps a private parlor might be more appropriate."

"No." Kate frowned at her sister for taking his side, irritated even more by Nora's flagrant attempt to pacify her by employing a pet name. "I am infinitely more comfortable out here. No matter what the rest of you decide, I shall remain here in the common room."

Lord Colter had the effrontery to catch her arm as if she were his little sister or an errant child. "Do try and be sensible, Kate."

Oh, how she hated it when he used that phrase on her.

"Is this fellow troubling you?" Lord Weatherford tapped Lord Colter on the shoulder. "These ladies are my guests, sir, and I must ask you to unhand the young lady and step aside."

Before Kate could explain to their protective host, Greyson spun around and faced the intruder. He stepped back as if slapped. "Weatherford?"

Lord Weatherford's perfect features twisted in a vicious sneer. "*Colter.*"

Greyson braced himself like a faithful watchdog facing off against a badger. "What are *you* doing here?"

"Might ask the same question of you, except I don't care." When Greyson refused to back down, Lord Weatherford took a small step forward and glared up at Lord Colter. "If you must know, Lady Alameda is a close personal friend of mine. I invited her and her lovely nieces to dine with me. So, I'll thank you to take yourself off, laddie."

"Laddie?" Tilly stared up at Kate's towering former fiancé.

Instead of backing away, Greyson leaned forward, menacingly, over Lord Weatherford. "I think not."

Weatherford didn't back down either. "Go away, Colter. You're not wanted here. Find a cave or, better yet, a church to hide in. Isn't that where you *holier-than-thou* hermits prefer to spend your time? Now, if you'll excuse me, these ladies are awaiting my company."

Lord Colter refused to let him by. "The likes of you can have nothing to do with these young ladies."

"Still the same pompous boor you were in school, I see. I taught you a lesson in manners then, boy, and don't think I won't do it again if you force my hand."

Lord Colter pressed ever closer, taking full advantage of his height. "I'm not twelve anymore. You'll find it considerably more difficult to bully me now."

Kate gulped down a dry-throated lump of uneasiness, and began to doubt the wisdom of accepting Lord Weatherford's hospitality.

"You are unfit company," Lord Colter continued in a low menacing tone. "If these ladies knew what a double-dealing cockalorum you were, they would have nothing to do with you."

Lord Weatherford's expression iced over at those words. The situation turned so chaotic, Kate instinctively stepped back, scarcely able to breathe.

Lord Weatherford pulled a pistol out of his coat pocket. He cocked back the hammer and pointed it directly at Lord Colter's lovely patrician nose.

"Greyson!" Kate's cry was muffled by her simultaneous gasp.

"No!" Tilly screamed.

Nora yanked Tilly back and clutched her tight. Sadie grasped Aunt Honore's arm, shouting, "Do something! Stop them."

"Hush, child." Honore patted Sadie's hand. "Mustn't ever get between two bears."

Lord Weatherford's voice remained low and steady. "Apologize, Colter, or I shall be forced to rearrange your features."

Greyson, rather than standing down, braced himself in front of his opponent. "Or what? You'll shoot me in a room full of witnesses? It would be worth it to see a blackguard like you hang."

Lord Weatherford's grip on the pistol tightened. "In that scenario, it's rather unlikely you'd be able to attend."

"Debatable, given your aim. Should you manage to do the deed, I'll enjoy the view from above. While you, *Lord Ignoramus*, shall dance at the end of a rope and spend eternity rotting in hell."

And to think, Greyson had accused *her* of being sharp-tongued.

Fear nearly gagged her, but Kate's lips finally parted in alarm. "No. No. Stop this, gentlemen. Stop. Now." Her warning went unheeded.

Lord Weatherford's jaw tensed. His lips pressed into taut thin lines, and his eyes screwed up into tiny aiming slits.

He was going to shoot.

The man was so enraged that his fingers quivered. A premonition flooded Kate's mind. Lord Colter's face: a hole where his beautiful, straight nose ought to be, and blood streaming down his white cravat. But the worst part—the most unbearable part—was the blank, empty look that suddenly overtook his eyes. This unthinkable future came to her in a horrible, blinding flash.

She couldn't bear it.

Before thought or reason could stop her, Kate lurched for the gun.

"Noooo!" poured from her lips in an elongated, guttural cry, as if time distorted her vocal cords. That split second stretched into terrifying eternity. Kate flew forward, grabbing Lord Weatherford's upraised arm and shoving it aside.

A shot splintered the air, ricocheting against her ears. Everything vibrated. It was as if a gargantuan hammer struck the earth.

Greyson fell back.

Kate stumbled forward onto her knees. Both men gaped at her as if the same ringing that thrummed through her head pounded through theirs as well.

"What have you done?" Lord Weatherford stared at his gun knocked to the floor, its barrel smoldering. Sulphuric vapors and acrid burnt powder stung everyone's eyes. "You've killed him."

"No!" Kate coughed and tried to wave away the biting smoke. "No, I saved—"

Saved him.

Hadn't she?

She scrambled to Greyson. He lay slumped against the table leg, his hands smeared with red, a dark stain spreading on his coat, and blood spilling onto the floor. Through the haze, he looked over at her, his eyes wide with shock.

As if far, far away, Kate heard people screaming.

Shouting.

The room began to spin and tilt in a very peculiar fashion. "Oh, for pity's saaa—"

A black whirling stupor pulled her to the ground.

Chapter 7
The Shot Heard 'Round the Inn

K ATE AWOKE TO the caustic scent of smelling salts stinging her nose. She sputtered and pushed away her aunt's hand.

Where was she?

Oh yes, the inn. Lord Colter had been shot. And had she fainted? "No," she groaned. What an utterly useless thing to do, when he could be—*oh heavens!*

She leaned up and pushed her aunt aside to see where Lord Colter lay slumped against the table leg. He was sitting up holding his arm.

Not dead.

But most definitely in need of care. Why was no one doing anything? She caught hold of her aunt's wrist. "Have you sent for a physician?"

Aunt Honore pulled away and brushed off her sleeve. "I've had my hands quite full trying to revive you. *He is not my* responsibility."

"Thank God for that." Lord Colter muttered sardonically. In a more irritated tone, he addressed Kate. "There's no need for a doctor. I'm fine. It's only a flesh wound."

Kate surveyed the blood staining his clothes and pooling on the floor. It required every ounce of her willpower not to recoil. "Don't be daft. It is obviously more serious than that. Not to mention, people die from flesh wounds every day."

"Do they now?" Aunt Honore asked, as if she found her niece highly amusing. "And you would know this because...?"

Kate got to her feet, wobbled a bit, and braced herself on a nearby chair. Nora rushed to Kate and supported her. "Steady on. Perhaps you should sit."

"No. As soon as my ears stop ringing, I'll be fine." She clasped her sister's hand. It took a few seconds before Kate had full control of her faculties. As soon as her equilibrium and good sense returned, she shook out her rumpled skirts and turned to the spectators gathering around them. "A physician!" she shouted. "Innkeeper! We are in need of a physician!"

The innkeeper stood amongst his guests, frowning at the hole in his wall and the blood on his floor. He lifted a finger. "I hear ye. Seems to me, what we're needing 'twould be a maid to mop up this mess." The gentility in his speech had completely vanished. His thick brows knit together as he stared at Lord Weatherford's gun. "That, and a magistrate to arrest this fellow."

"It was an accident!" Lord Weatherford edged back, picked up his pistol, and shoved it in his pocket. "A misunderstanding. The ruddy thing never would've gone off if this young lady hadn't—"

Kate had heard enough. "Send someone for a physician, innkeeper. Immediately! Lest you want this gentleman to die on your premises."

"Don't be silly, Kate. I'm not going to die." Lord Colter tried to rise but failed in the effort and thumped back to a sitting position. He hung his head for a second before tugging at his cravat and untying it. "The only service I need is for someone to help me bind up my arm."

"Now who's being stubborn?" She snatched the cloth away from him, doubled it over, and wrapped it around Lord Colter's upper arm, tying it snugly enough to staunch the bleeding but not so tight that it cut off his circulation. "Innkeeper, if you are not going to procure a physician for us, would you be so good as to point out Lord Colter's private parlor?"

With a disapproving sniff and a mumbled derogatory phrase about the behavior of some members of the *quality*, their host pointed to a door at the far end of the coffee room.

"Excellent." Kate forced a smile. "Now, if you would also ask a maid to bring a pot of hot water and a bottle of whiskey if you have it. You may add the latter to Lord Weatherford's bill." She turned to that gentleman. "And you, my lord, do you plan to stand there with your mouth hanging open like a codfish? Or will you help me move your victim to his private parlor?"

"My victim?" The codfish shoved a chair aside and stooped down to help her. "He's *your* victim. You were the one who made the gun go off."

"I'm not dead, you know. I'm right here," Lord Colter grumbled. "And I'm nobody's victim."

Kate and Lord Weatherford paid him no heed. She was busy

trying to determine what part of Greyson's anatomy to grasp without jarring his injured arm. She stopped long enough to rebut the insolent gentleman to whom they owed all this trouble. "You were the one pointing a gun at him. I was simply trying to keep you from killing him. Get under his good arm." She waved Weatherford into position. "That's right, the arm you didn't put a bullet through. Very good. There, that's it."

"I can get myself up," Greyson protested.

She sniffed at his bravado. "If you do that, my lord, judging by your pallor, you'll fall straight over and crack your head open. Don't you think you've made enough of a mess for one day?"

She signaled to Weatherford, clutched a fistful of Greyson's waistcoat with her left hand, and wrapped her right arm around his waist. "On my count. Ready? One, two, three."

With a groan, some precarious tipping, and a bit of shuffling, they assisted Lord Colter to his feet.

"Young ladies are not supposed to bark orders," Lord Weatherford muttered. "And they are most certainly not supposed to interfere in an argument between two gentlemen." He continued to lecture her while practically dragging Lord Colter between tables as they headed for the parlor. "Especially when there is a weapon involved."

This pistol-wielding dandy would have to do better than that if he intended to pin the blame on her.

"And *gentlemen*—" Kate said, emphasizing the word so that he would know she harbored serious doubts in that quarter, "—are not supposed to point firearms at people's heads." She was getting blood stains on her traveling frock and it was all his fault. "Especially not in a coaching inn, when everyone's nerves are already frayed."

"Ha!" Lord Weatherford had the unmitigated gall to scoff at her. "I doubt you've ever had a frayed nerve in your life. I'll wager you've a will of iron." He tugged Greyson's arm higher across his shoulders.

Their victim groaned. "Have a care, mate."

"I'm not your mate," Weatherford sneered. "Not by a long-shot. If it were up to me, I'd have left you to bleed to death on the floor. I'm only helping now because if I didn't, Miss Termagant over there would ring a peal over my head." He glared sideways at Kate. "Has anyone ever told you that you're a peculiar sort of young lady?"

Lord Colter snorted. "Careful what you say. She's apt to bite your ear off and spit it in your face."

Her mouth opened in search of a suitable retort but Lord Weatherford beat her to it.

"No doubt. She's not like any female I ever met before. Ought to have been born a field marshal."

Kate ground her teeth together. It was enough of a struggle to move Lord Colter, the great lumbering ox, without having to put up with their joint antagonism. "These pretty compliments are turning my head, gentlemen," she said in a sugary tone, but ground out her next words on a rumbly millstone. "But I must ask you to kindly refrain from talking."

Lord Weatherford did not heed her warning. Instead, he addressed Lord Colter. "What is she to you, anyway?" Curiosity laced the question, and he leaned out to peer studiously at Kate. "She's not your sister. No resemblance that I can see—"

Lord Colter nearly choked. "Definitely *not* my sister. Thank the Maker."

"A cousin, then?"

If Greyson told Lord Weatherford the truth, that he and Kate had been engaged but he'd cast her aside because of her foul temperament, her debut in London society would be tainted from the start. "Nothing!" she blurted. "I'm nothing to him. Nothing at all. We're not related. Not even friends. We grew up in the same village. Mere acquaintances. That's all."

Lord Colter twisted sideways to deliver a pointed frown at Kate, and in the process bumped his head on the low doorway. He winced, and through clinched teeth said, "Her father is a family friend."

A plain pine table stood in the center of the room. It would have to do. They would never be able to haul him upstairs to a bed. "Sit him on the table. Help me remove his coat. We can use that under his head."

Greyson rumbled unhappily as she rolled it up. "Might've mended that."

"It was too far gone. Now stop fussing and lie down." She placed it carefully under his head and helped him recline on the table. He caught her wrist, surprising her with a grieved expression, and quietly asked, "Am I nothing to you? I would've said we were *friends*. At least that."

A wave of remorse nearly drowned her. It was true. They *were* friends. Weren't they? After all, he'd known her since she was a babe in leading strings. Except friends didn't jilt one another in front of everyone they'd known their whole lives. Certainly not in front of one's whole village. And yet—

"Friends?" Lord Weatherford overheard Greyson and

nodded. "Makes sense. Else why would she risk her life trying to save your sorry arse?" He glanced sideways at her.

Thankfully, Kate's sisters and Aunt Honore hurried in, bursting apart that awkward moment. "Is he going to die?" Tilly asked, but Nora tugged her back.

"Not if I can help it." Kate tore away what was left of Greyson's white cotton sleeve.

Lord Colter glanced at Tilly and shook his head. "You must all stop being so maudlin. I'm not going to die. The bullet only grazed my arm."

Sadie gasped at the sight of his wound and edged back against the wall.

Tilly, on the other hand, drew nearer with morbid interest. "All the same, one must be careful. Wounds can get infected, then fever sets in, and—"

"Hush! I need to concentrate." Kate confiscated a dishtowel from the sideboard and carefully blotted blood away from the gory ditch marring Greyson's shoulder.

Nora grimaced and turned away, covering Tilly's eyes. The younger girl escaped her sister's protective hands and studied the lengthy gash. "Why is it blackened like that?"

"Burn marks from the bullet." Kate gently examined how deep it was and checked the ragged, torn flesh. "It needs to be cleaned up and stitched."

"Agreed." Tilly pursed her lips inspecting the wound.

A maid rushed in, carrying the requested pot of hot steaming water. She set it on the sideboard along with a bottle of whiskey. "Oye!" She grimaced when she saw Lord Colter's arm and scurried from the room.

Kate turned to Lord Weatherford. "My lord, go and find the innkeeper. If he has not sent for a physician, you must procure directions to the nearest doctor and ride with all haste to fetch him here. Meanwhile, I will clean the wound and do my best to stave off infection."

"Must I? You're doing more than most sawbones will do. Can't you stitch it?"

"With what?" Kate raised her hands in wonderment at his unwillingness to cooperate.

"A needle and thread, I should think. Surely one of you young ladies have a piece of embroidery string." He smiled charmingly at Nora. "A local doctor isn't likely to do any better than that."

"Don't be ridiculous." Kate glared at him. "A doctor will have catgut for properly closing a wound."

"No need." Lord Colter propped himself up and tried to inspect his arm. "I told you before, I don't need a doctor. Last thing I want is a bowl of leeches draining the life out of me. It's merely a small—"

When he took a closer look at his wound, his face blanched. He sagged back and his head thudded against the rolled-up coat.

"Go! Fetch a doctor! Now!" Kate clapped her hands at Lord Weatherford, the way one shoos a naughty goat out of the garden. "And you'd best hurry. Unless you prefer to hang for murder?"

"Aye-aye, General." Lord Weatherford mocked her with a salute. Much to Kate's embarrassment, he took an overlong moment to look her over appreciatively. "You know," he said, in an almost flirtatious manner, "no one likes a managing chit." Why did he say it with that absurd tone as if he meant the opposite?

Chit.

She detested that term. She was not a child. Nor was she kitten-like. Kate fought an overpowering urge to smack him with Greyson's bloody bandages. Instead, she drew in a steadying breath. "If you think I am unaware of the fact that I have a sharp tongue, my lord, you are sorely mistaken. Now, stop dilly-dallying, and hurry along to fetch a physician."

Aunt Honore, who had remained surprisingly silent during this entire fiasco, propped herself against a small cupboard near the window. "I take it all back. I can see now that you're the one who ought to be named after me. It's decided. You shall be my protégé."

Before Kate could respond to this dubious honor, the innkeeper blocked the doorway, halting Lord Weatherford. "Not so fast."

He had two large footmen at his heels, fellows who probably doubled as stable hands from the rustic look of them. "You lot are disrupting the other guests. Paying guests, same as you. I can't have that. Bad for business. I'll be asking ye to take yer leave as soon as possible."

"Leave? What!" Kate's voice jumped an octave in alarm. "No. We arranged to stay the night. And Lord Colter is mortally wounded. You can't—"

"I can. An' I will." The innkeeper huffed loudly. "I thought it through, I 'ave. You'll do as I say; elsewise, I'll call in the magistrate and have the lot of you hauled off to jail. You can't go shooting holes in m' walls and frightening off the folk in the public rooms. Puts 'em off the place." His chest puffed out. "I won't have it! The magistrate is a good friend to this establishment, seeing as he's who I pays me rents to, and neither of us wants our good name tarnished. So, you folks had best move on your way."

"Well, it simply is not possible—not until this man sees a doctor." Kate wiped the blood from her finger. "If we move him now, you will be as responsible for his death as that gentleman there. And I will see that charges are brought up against you. My father is a magistrate as well."

That made the innkeeper take a step back.

Kate pressed her advantage. "Now, if you will be so good as to give Lord Weatherford directions to your village doctor?"

"I doubt the fellow what shot 'im ought to be trusted to bring a sawbones." The innkeeper sized up Lord Weatherford. "Nay, he'll make a run for it, if he knows what's good fer 'im."

"Nothing of the kind." Weatherford puffed out his chest. "I've done nothing wrong. Furthermore, I'm a gentleman. And a gentleman does not '*make a run fer it*.' Now, kindly give me those directions, and I shall fetch the doctor as Miss Linnet has so delicately commanded me to do."

The innkeeper grunted and signaled to one of the burly fellows standing behind him to go with Lord Weatherford and show him the way.

Aunt Honore stood digging through her pelisse for something in its depths. Kate prayed it would not be another gun. Her aunt was famous for carrying a pistol in her purse. Instead, Honore pulled out two gold half-guineas. "This ought to cover your trouble for patching the hole in your wall."

She tossed one coin to him and he caught it without blinking an eye.

"And this," she held up the remaining half-guinea, letting it catch the light from the window. "This is for an extra flagon of ale and cakes for each of the tables out in your coffee room. That ought to calm your guests. We shall take our leave as soon as our horses are rested and a physician has attended this gentleman. In exchange, you will forget you ever heard my name or Lord *Welterbasket's* in conjunction with this incident."

The innkeeper stared lustfully at the golden coin in her fingers and itched his gray side-whiskers. "Don't ye mean Lord Weatherf—"

"Tch!" Honore held a finger to her lips shushing him. "I'm paying you to forget."

"Oh, aye." He nodded and winked. "Aye. And I 'ave your word you'll be on yer way as soon as the lad there is stitched up?"

"Certainly. And after my nieces and I have had some refreshments."

He tugged on his forelock, agreeing to her demands, and Aunt Honore tossed him the second coin.

Kate turned to her aunt as soon as the innkeeper was out of earshot. "What are we to do? Lord Colter won't be in any condition to travel today."

Honore shrugged. "I don't see how that's any concern of mine."

Kate dabbed warm water mixed with whiskey to clean out the wound. Greyson winced. "Those ragged edges are going to have to be cut away." She stood and wiped her fingers on the last clean corner of the rag and addressed the maid. "I'll need more rags and a very sharp knife."

Once the items were supplied, she set to work despite Greyson's protests. "Don't you think we ought to wait for the doctor? What do you know about dressing a gunshot?"

She slapped his hand away and went to work. "I've trimmed plenty of roasts and turkeys in my time and cleaned enough skinned knees, scrapes, and cuts to know that if we want to prevent infection, this scorched flesh has got to go."

"Hhmm. Roasts and skinned knees. Builds your confidence, doesn't it, my lord?" Lady Alameda poured another whiskey and approached their patient. He reached out his hand to take the glass, but Honore winced at the sight of his wound and tossed the amber liquid down her own throat.

Kate saw his fallen countenance and filled the bottom of a glass for him. "This may help take the edge off. Although I doubt you'll feel much. That tissue is burnt so badly the feeling will be gone from it." He gulped the contents.

Kate set to work.

"You needn't worry. She has a knack for it." Tilly patted Greyson's hand as he held the table with a white-knuckled grip. "She's fixed me up on more than one occasion."

Kate gently pared away Lord Colter's burnt skin. "There. That's done it." She stepped back, wiped her brow with her forearm, took a deep breath, and dumped more whiskey over the gash.

Lord Colter roared like an injured lion and issued several unrepeatable oaths.

Kate turned to her aunt and resumed her debate. "I'm quite certain Lord Colter won't be able to drive his phaeton. Not today or for several days."

Her aunt gave her an indifferent shrug. "I fail to see why that matters to us. Let him find his own way home. Isn't he the same fellow who publicly broke your—"

"Aunt!" Kate warned, far too sternly. She desperately hoped no one outside the parlor had overheard. And then there was Greyson, listening far too closely. Kate needed to divert everyone's attention, and she knew exactly how to do that.

A stern lecture.

"Aunt," she began, with forced calm, "surely you've heard of the Good Samaritan? It is your duty to care for your fellow man, whether 'tis an enemy or a friend. We cannot leave anyone to die or suffer alone. Surely, the good Lord will punish those who abandon the helpless and reward those who render mercy to those in need. No matter how wretched, or aggravating, or rude the person in need might be—"

"Hey," Lord Colter objected, "who are you calling wretched?"

"Oh, I didn't mean *you* were wretched." She bent over him and smoothed his hair back. "It was the *aggravating* and *rude* parts that were intended for you."

"Oh, good heavens." Aunt Honore swallowed more whiskey and squeezed her eyes closed as it burned down her throat. "Are you quite finished sermonizing, child? Because I don't like being preached at. God gave up on me a long time ago, and I suggest you do the same." She swirled the amber liquid and, with one arched brow, glared at Kate.

Kate didn't respond. She studied the stained floor-boards. No doubt she would be sermonizing again before the day was over. It was her way. She was plagued with a caustic tongue, always correcting people, always giving orders. She'd been doing it since . . . well, ever since her mama had abandoned her.

Died.

And left her with three little sisters to raise.

Lord Colter reached for her hand, but she didn't take it.

"Are you listening to me?" Aunt Honore's voice echoed around the room so loudly it made Kate's head snap up. "I expect an answer, Kate. What do you want me to do about this—" She waved her hand indicating Greyson. "This gigantic, aggravating wretch?"

"Don't forget *rude*," Tilly added.

"Yes, indeed. Rude." Aunt Honore crossed her arms frowning expectantly at Kate.

What did she want?

She'd so seldom been asked that question.

_Chapter 8
What Did She Want?

A FRIGHTFULLY THORNY question.

What did she want?

Kate squeezed her eyes shut and rubbed her temple in a vain attempt to escape the flurry of responses buzzing around her head.

It was Nora, *dear, sweet, gentle* Nora, who interrupted Kate's whirling thoughts and suggested, "Could we not bring him with us? Lady Alameda's coach is well-sprung and comfortable. If Lord Colter were to rest his head on your shoulder, Kate, there might be enough room."

"Um . . ." Kate said eloquently.

Nora glanced around the room, no doubt counting and mentally seating all of those present, and amended her suggestion. "Perhaps Lord Weatherford might be prevailed upon to ferry one or two of us in his carriage—that way, there would be enough room for Lord Colter to rest comfortably across the seat."

"I don't know." Kate turned nervously to Lord Colter. He'd tilted his head and appeared to be listening attentively, but hurriedly closed his eyes. No help in that quarter. "Aunt? What do you think? Would it be possible to transport him? We can't leave him here. Not in this condition."

"You mean to put this rude wretch and his bleeding shoulder on my good, calf-leather seats?" Aunt Honore took several huffy breaths before finally putting up her hands. "Very well. Spare me your lectures." She waved away Kate's pleas. "I suppose we must play the Samaritan. However, I can't allow any of you green girls to ride in a carriage alone with that rascal Weatherford. Your father would skin me alive. So I shall sacrifice my comfort and accompany Sadie and Tilly in Naughty Neddy's rig. But you will owe me for this, young lady. His seats won't be nearly as comfortable and—"

"Naughty Ned!" Lord Colter suddenly appeared to be wide awake. "You knew his reputation! You knew all along that Weatherford was a reprobate?"

"A reprobate? Tch-tch, I never said that. He is a spirited young fellow, that's all. Too spirited for girls as green as these."

"Spirited, my arse," Lord Colter grumped. "He's a scoundrel. Unfit company for any young lady. What's more, you can't excuse his behavior with youth. He's not young. He's five years my senior."

"Oh my!" Honore smirked. "Nearly one foot in the grave."

Kate stopped chewing her lip and fretting about enduring the prolonged proximity to her former fiancé during the carriage ride to London in order to protest something Greyson had said earlier, "I'm not green."

"You are too!" Lord Colter grimaced in an effort to lean up and frown at Kate

"Green as a newborn chick," Honore chuckled.

"Chicks aren't green, Aunt." Tilly sounded genuinely confused.

"Who's green?" Lord Weatherford barged into the room with the doctor in tow.

Kate would prefer no one answer that question and so she quickly took charge. "Ah, Doctor. You are much needed. Here, come and see." She took his elbow and guided him to their patient. "I have cut away the excess skin and cleaned the wound with whiskey, but obviously it will need stitches. Now, how else may I assist you?"

"Well . . ." he adjusted his glasses and pinched his lips upon inspecting Greyson's shoulder. "You might pour me a glass of that whiskey you mentioned."

Aunt Honore handed him a tumbler, and when he turned to accept it, he frowned at the number of females staring at him. "I daresay these young ladies ought not watch the procedure. Gels have a tendency to run squeamish, if you catch my meaning."

Aunt Honore merely lifted her glass.

"Not these girls." Lord Weatherford hung his greatcoat on a hook.

Tilly nodded. "He's right, you know. My sister has dressed any number of pigs, and I am vastly interested in gruesome things."

"Are you now?" The doctor frowned at Tilly as if she were a rabbit tromping through his garden.

"Your bag, Doctor." Kate handed him his worn leather satchel. "Would you like me to thread the needle for you?"

He snatched it from her and adjusted his spectacles. "No, thank you, miss. I can thread my own needles." He opened the bag and unrolled a length of cloth fitted with various instruments. Selecting a curved needle, he held it up to the light from the window.

"Shouldn't you clean it first? There's still blood on it. I can see it from here." Not that Kate was very far away from it. Indeed, her nose was near enough to the instrument to note it was covered in far too much reddish-brown grime. "Here. Give it to me and I shall clean it for you." She snapped her fingers and opened her palm.

"Listen here, young lady, a little dried blood never hurt anyone, and may I remind you that I am the doctor, and you—"

Lord Colter interrupted with a loud grumbly sigh. "You may as well give her a task to do. Otherwise, she'll be hanging over your shoulder directing every stitch."

The doctor looked at Kate, frowned harshly, took another swig of whiskey, and dropped the needle in her waiting palm.

"And the catgut?" she asked with a pleasant smile.

He glanced heavenward and handed her the spool. "I shall just sit here and rest my feet, shall I?"

"As you wish. As I explained to our friend earlier, had I the proper tools, I could've done the job without sending for you. I've stitched up many a goose to secure the stuffing."

"Have you now?" The good doctor plopped in a chair and waved his hand. "Well, far be it from me to stop so superbly qualified a person as yourself. It's been a long enough day for me, what with enduring nine hours of screaming whilst delivering Mrs. Thompson's baby, then rushing to Sandy Farm to set Eric Culpepper's broken arm—squirmy little devil—and straight after that, on to the parsonage to tend Pastor Woodford's infected toe. I could use a rest. Stitch away, young lady. Stitch away. I suppose if you can sew up a Christmas goose, closing that wee wound ought to be a picnic."

Kate did not care for his sarcastic tone, but she chose to ignore it, cleaning the needle and threading it proficiently. Doctor or not, she didn't trust a fellow ready to employ such a filthy needle. Greyson was better off in her care.

She approached her former fiancé, armed and ready to do battle with his injury, but Greyson turned a bit pale. "Here now, Kate, don't you think, perhaps, it would be better if—"

"Now, Lord Colter," she clucked her tongue in a mild scold. "You must be brave and hold very still," she warned. "Do you need me to call the innkeeper's stablemen to hold you down?"

"I'll do it." Lord Weatherford jumped up and offered to help with altogether too much glee. "I'll hold the blighter down."

Greyson growled. He'd been growling more than usual today, she observed. Through clamped teeth, he warned Naughty Ned, "Touch me and, so help me, I'll plow your face into the next kingdom."

Kate sniffed peevishly. "That's no way to talk, my lord. 'No, thank you,' would've sufficed."

"This should be good." With a rude snicker, Lord Weatherford slapped two shillings on the table. "Care to take odds, Doc, on the gentleman's chances of survival? A crown says Colter gets gangrene."

The doctor chuckled. "Nah, I reckon the lad will pull through. The gel, though, is a different matter."

"Queasy? No, not her, Doc." Ned snickered. "She's an iron-hearted maiden if ever there was one."

"I'll take that wager and give you two to one." The doctor plucked a few coins from his pocket and shook them in his palm.

"Done!" Ned leaned over to grin at Kate. "Do me proud, Miss Termagant." He pulled back, frowning. "Hhmm. Well, I'll be frog-snockered. She does look a bit peaked." Nincompoop Ned retreated to the windowsill, his nose twitching nervously as he passed by his coins on the table.

"Enough!" Kate snapped. "If everyone would *please* refrain from speculating. I need to concentrate."

She pursed her lips and edged closer to Greyson, leaning over the task at hand. *It's no different than sewing up a Christmas goose,* she told herself.

Just like a Christmas goose.

Except it wasn't.

Not at all.

His skin wasn't grayish-pink, nor was it stretchy and bird-like with ugly little nubbins where the feathers had once been. No, this was Lord Colter's alluring smooth shoulder. Warm and alive beneath her fingers. And she could hear his heart beating.

Pounding.

Or was that hers?

His lips clamped into a worried line as he watched her take aim.

She swallowed—*tried* to swallow, except her throat had gone dry. She gritted her teeth and pushed the needle into his beautiful warm skin. Blood bubbled up around it.

Goose skin never did that.

Kate winced.

It was one thing to cut away dead skin, but it was quite another to stab her needle into Greyson and make him bleed. To wound him afresh. His crimson blood trailed onto her fingers and ran down, flowing in streams onto his already stained shirt. This close, the metallic tang of it nearly choked her.

Hot.

Why had it suddenly gotten so confounded hot in the parlor? Sweat dampened her neck. She tried to blink away her blurry vision, but it wouldn't unblur. And for some reason, the room was getting darker.

"Light," she muttered. "I need more liiigh—"

Oh bollywogs!

Not *again.*

Kate awoke to chattering voices and her sisters leaning over her. Nora brushed back her hair and in a soothing voice explained, "You fell and hit your head, Katie. Hold still, I'm applying a cold compress to the bump—"

But she couldn't sit still, not when . . .

"Lord Colter! I have to—" She bolted upright, only to find she had been draped indecorously across three chairs.

"No need. The doctor is tending to him." Sadie smiled. "He told Lord Weatherford he's going to charge double for having to look after you."

"Don't see why," grumbled Lord Weatherford. "Made an extra four shillings off my bet. And it's all your fault, my dear Miss Linnet. This whole fandangle is your doing."

"Fandango," Tilly corrected.

"Fandangle sounds better. More like the ruddy mess it is. Either way, it's all her fault."

Tilly's little chin lifted, and she nodded with altogether too much of a know-everything expression. "He does have a point."

Was it Kate's fault?

She'd only meant to help. To save his sorry behind, or rather to save his irritatingly stubborn, albeit mildly handsome, face from having a hole blown through it—

"Oh, do be quiet, Tilly." Kate lay back down.

Her head hurt something fierce, and she had decisions to make. That ill-tempered doctor had better be doing a decent job of stitching up Greyson, or . . .

Or what?

What would she do exactly? And why did it matter? What difference did it make if a grisly scar marred Greyson's shoulder? Why should she care? It was none of her business. It didn't matter in the least.

Although, if Lord Colter were to contract gangrene and lose a limb, or worse, *his* life—well, naturally, everyone would be overset about that. Kate would be no different than anyone else in Clapsforth-on-Wye. The entire village would be grieved. And she would make sure that incompetent old fool of a doctor never touched another soul with his filthy needles again.

Not that it mattered.

It didn't. What's more, the farther she stayed away from Lord Colter, the better it would be for her—for everyone concerned. Riding back in the carriage with him leaning his head against her shoulder was completely unacceptable. From here on out, Miss Kate Linnet intended to keep her distance from the man who had ruined her life.

She sat up with renewed determination. He may have ruined things for her in Clapsforth-on-Wye, but she was not going to let him ruin her plans for London.

"Aunt," she said, in the sweetest tone she could muster, "I believe I would prefer to ride in Lord Weatherford's carriage for the remainder of the journey."

"What!" Aunt Honore shot back sharply.

"What?" Sadie echoed rudely, her mouth gaping like a goldfish. "With Naughty Ned?"

Greyson pushed the doctor aside. "No! Absolutely not."

Even Nora joined the choir of naysayers. "Would that be proper, Katie, dearest? His reputation does seem to be—pardon my saying so, my lord—somewhat questionable."

Naughty Ned jumped down from his perch on the windowsill. "Oh, I say. Setting these slanderous insults aside, I don't recall inviting any of you into my equipage." He glared at Kate, but then his expression slowly turned wicked. "Hhmm. Although, being a gentleman, I suppose I've no choice but to comply. If you insist—"

Lord Colter grasped the doctor's stitching hand and sat up. "She doesn't insist! She suffered a blow to her head, and obviously, the young lady isn't thinking straight. Kate, do be sensible." At her haughty sniff, he turned his appeal to Aunt Honore. "Lady Alameda, you cannot allow this."

"Can't I?" Aunt Honore, who Kate knew disliked anyone telling her what she could or couldn't do, drew back and bristled. "I don't see the harm." She turned quite smug, crossing her arms and stubbornly lifting her chin. "In fact, I shall be riding with Dear Neddy, too. There, you see? They shall be properly chaperoned."

"Oh dear," Nora moaned softly and looked at all of them desperately. "Then who will care for Lord Colter on the road to London?"

Aunt Honore flipped her hand, flicking away Nora's query. "You younger girls can see to that."

Dr. Simeon huffed loudly. "Young man, lie back and hold still, would you? I'm almost finished." His patient complied. The doctor tied his last stitch and bit off the catgut with his teeth.

With his teeth!

"Scissors, Doctor. Use the scissors!" Kate roared at him. "Biting the catgut cannot be a sanitary practice."

Tilly tugged on Dr. Simeon's coat. "Is that stuff really made from cat guts?"

The ill-mannered physician peered down at Kate's beloved little sister as if Tilly were something the aforementioned cat had dragged in and deposited at his feet. He sniffed. "No, young lady. If you must know, this *stuff* is made of sheep intestines."

Before Kate could compose a proper set-down for the self-important old sot, Lord Colter started railing at her. "I'm going to tell your father, Kate. He won't be pleased about this sort of reckless behavior. You know he won't. Not when he hears about this blackguard's abominable reputation."

Lord Weatherford slammed his third glass of whiskey down on the table. "Why must everyone keep besmirching my reputation?"

Lady Alameda patted his shoulder. "I rather think you did that to yourself, Neddy dearest."

Kate narrowed a smug glare at Greyson. "And how is Papa to find out? You're in no condition to travel anywhere unaided."

Greyson's jaw flexed furiously for a full second. "I'll send a post."

Kate smiled serenely. "In which case, he won't hear about it until I'm already in London."

"Ha! She's got you there, old chap." Lord Weatherford lifted his glass to her.

"Shut it, Neddy." Greyson brooded.

Kate crossed her arms quite pleased with how upset Lord Colter appeared to be. "I'm traveling in the company of Lord Weatherford and my aunt and that's my final word on the subject."

Greyson's frown lifted and his back straightened. "In that case, I'm coming with you, too, Neddy, old man."

"What?" Naughty Ned looked ready to spit nails. "No! That is outside of enough. I won't—"

"Swallow your objections, Weatherford. You owe me this." Greyson's voice carried an abnormally hard tone—one that made Kate draw in a quick breath. "Otherwise, I will take you to court for this cock-up. I doubt the magistrates will look kindly upon you shooting a member of the peerage."

"But she . . . it was her—" Naughty Ned pointed at Kate.

"Said Adam about Eve, but God still held him accountable." Greyson's voice rumbled like a dray crushing limestone.

"Ahem," Dr. Simeon cleared his throat. "Keep those stitches dry and clean, young man. You'll need someone in London to remove them in two weeks or so. I daresay your young lady will attempt it if you can't find a proper physician."

"She's not *my* young lady."

"I most certainly am not!" Kate huffed.

"Balderol," muttered Aunt Honore.

Tilly, *who Kate dearly wished would stop correcting everyone*, chimed in. "I think our aunt means balderdash or folderol. I'm not certain which."

"Begging your pardon." The doctor bowed. "Begging *all* of your pardons. I should not have assumed *anyone* was *anyone's* young lady." He added a cheekish amount of eye-rolling, and smirked at all of them before turning to Lord Weatherford. "And I believe I'll take my payment now, if you don't mind."

"Send me a bill." Lord Weatherford frowned at the doctor as if he were completely balmy.

"Nay, my lord. That's not a gamble I'm willing to take. The way you're all carping at one another, I have serious doubts any of you will survive the trip to London."

While Lord Weatherford paid Dr. Simeon, Aunt Honore poured a cup of tea for her niece. "Here you are, my dear," she said in an uncharacteristically soothing tone. "You've been through a dreadfully stressful afternoon. Perhaps a cup of tea will restore your nerves."

Kate was about to protest that her nerves were perfectly fine, *thank you very much*, but she thought better of it. After all, this was an unusual show of affection coming from her aunt, and she wouldn't want to discourage such behavior.

She sipped it dutifully, noting that the tea tasted peculiar. The cream was a bit heavy, and it had too much sugar, but then her aunt was probably unaccustomed to preparing tea for herself. Being so frightfully rich, she probably relied too heavily upon maids to perform menial tasks such as . . . such as . . .

Kate rubbed her forehead. What was she about to say? Something about there being too much cream. Or was it too much sugar? Why was the room so wavy and watery?

She smiled warmly at Tilly, who had pushed her adorable little face up close to Kate's and asked, "What's wrong with your eyes, Kate? They look odd. Your pupils are as big as Ralphie's"

"Who in blazes is Ralphie?" asked Aunt Honore.

"Our spani—stop!" Tilly pushed Kate's hand away, when Kate was merely trying to pet Tilly's soft angelic curls.

"Spaniard?" Aunt Honore drew back in disbelief.

"Not a Spaniard, a spaniel. Our dog," Sadie explained and squinted intently at Kate. "Nora, come have a look. There is definitely something amiss with Katie's eyes."

Nonsense. Her eyes were fine. After all, Kate clearly saw Nora peering at her. Nora's lips moved and her mouth formed a funny O shape.

"Uh-oh. They're quite dilated."

Greyson swung off the table and rushed to Kate. "She must have a concussion."

"Nonsense." Aunt Honore shooed them all back. "Give the child some air. She just needs to lie down for a moment or two and rest her tongue."

"Her tongue?" Tilly chirped as Sadie dragged her aside. "You mean her head, don't you, Aunt?"

"Suit yourself." Aunt Honore shrugged, lowering Kate back down on the chairs. "Lie back and rest, my dear. That's right. There's a good girl." That done, Lady Alameda brushed her hands off on her skirts and turned to Kate's sisters. "For pity's sake! What a trial you all are. Don't make me waste any more laudanum on the rest of you."

To which everyone in the room glanced suspiciously at the vessels from which they'd been drinking.

Chapter 9
Oh, What Heavenly ... er ... Foul Dreams Are These?

A BUMP IN THE ROAD jarred Kate. No matter. She snuggled closer against Greyson's warm chest, relishing his strong arm around her shoulder. When had she ever felt so coddled, so cared for, so perfectly content? She was enjoying such a lovely dream that it seemed a shame to trouble oneself with waking up.

And why should she?

Kate breathed deep, luxuriating in rare contentment. Swimming in blissful oblivion, she felt no need to fret about her battered reputation in Clapsforth, nor did she have to strategize about navigating London society. It was delightfully simple here in dreamland, ever so peaceful, and—

The carriage jolted over a deep pothole and sent her flopping against the aforementioned chest in her dreamworld. Lord Colter groaned—a wincing sort of noise that could not possibly be part of any comfortable sleeping state.

Kate managed to pry one heavy eyelid open only to find herself surrounded by creaking and swaying and the darkness of a closed carriage. Furthermore, her cheek was resting on a rather damp, curdled shirt. A caustic tang emanated from the fine linen fabric. It smelled of blood, and unless she missed her foggy-headed guess, the dampness might be, at least partially, composed of her drool.

No.

This couldn't possibly be real.

Kate's other eyelid popped open rather more quickly than the first had done.

Oh, but it was. Her nose wrinkled in confirmation. *Utterly and mortifyingly real.*

She was, indeed, pressed up against a considerable amount of sticky drool. And, undoubtedly, the shirt in question belonged to her former fiancé. Her limbs were not as cooperative as her eyelids had been, or she would have immediately released her grip on his person. Nor did her mouth readily cooperate. A strange sound emerged, something like, "Gaahhh!"

"Sleeping Beauty awakens." Kate recognized *that* voice. Sarcasm packaged so neatly could only belong to Sadie.

The chest on which her head rested rumbled. Lord Colter was chuckling—at her expense. That galvanized her. She inhaled deeply, filling her livid lungs to the brim with musty, stale air, and pushed away from him. That wasn't good enough. She wiped her cheek and scooted as far across Aunt Honore's leather seats as the carriage would allow.

"Is she having a nightmare?" Tilly sounded worried.

"Umph." Sadie, on the other hand, didn't seem worried at all. "Maybe."

"Wh-where's Aunt Honore?" Kate's words came out garbled, thick and sludgy, like pea soup left out overnight.

Tilly bounced forward on the seat opposite her. "She's in the fancy carriage with Nora and Lord Weather*vane*."

"Wea-ther-*ford*." Kate slurred in an attempt to correct her baby sister.

"Yes, I know. Except you mustn't say so." Tilly dove into a head-rattling explanation. "While we were helping him carry you to the carriage, our aunt instructed us to forget his real name. When I asked how we ought to refer to him in the future, she said we ought not refer to him at all. First-rate scoundrel, she said. It would be better if no one knew that we knew him. When I explained that the occasion might arise, as it just did, in which it was necessary to refer to him, she said, '*Oh, for heaven's sake, call him something else. Call him Lord Biscuits for all I care, but do not use his real name.*'"

"He-he carried me?" Kate tucked her skirts around herself, envisioning the indelicacies of such a procedure.

Sadie snorted ungraciously and crossed her arms. "How did you suppose you ended up here in the carriage? You were in no condition to walk."

Tilly patted Kate's knee. "It's all right, Katie. We didn't strain ourselves or anything. Lord Biscuits did most of the work."

This resulted in an unhappy grumble from Greyson.

Kate's vocal cords finally decided to behave properly. "Why are you peeved?"

Lord Colter adjusted to a more upright position. "It's on account of that insufferable scapegrace! I cannot tolerate how he insinuated himself into the situation. Nor the way he carried you in such an intimate fashion. Were I not injured, I would've thrashed him soundly."

Insufferable, insinuated, intimate, injured—there were far too many i's in Greyson's rant. Kate wasn't in the mood for backward poetry. She rubbed her temples, which were throbbing like the very devil. "It is a good thing you didn't, my lord. You would have torn open your stitches. And I suppose *someone* had to carry me. Would you have preferred one of the innkeeper's stable hands did so?"

"No, but—"

She waved his objections away before he could debate the issue. "More to the point, I was addressing my *sister*. Not you." She turned away from him. Not that she had dared to look at him directly in the face, not after slobbering all over him as she had done. Instead, she merely squinted in his general vicinity. Fortunately, the interior of the coach was fairly dark. Which meant that sometime during her driveling delirium, night had fallen upon them, and she'd lain against his chest far longer than respectable etiquette allowed. What's worse, she'd been exceptionally comfortable doing so. How could that be?

It made no sense—none at all. He was annoying and . . .

Good heavens! The entire situation was completely unacceptable. If she'd had a proper chaperone instead of Aunt Honore, he would be forced to marry her simply because she'd soiled his shirt in such an intimate manner. A treacherous thought flitted through her head.

Would that be so bad?

Yes! It would be unthinkable to wed a man who thought so little of her, a man who would rather rot in hell, *as he so delicately phrased it*, than spend his life with her. Not to mention, she wanted no part of marriage and all it entailed—namely, more children and more responsibilities. No, she'd had quite enough of that, thank you very much.

She refused to give that whole absurd scenario another thought. Aside from that, she had bigger fish to debone. Specifically, her sister's peevish scowl.

"Sadie, dearest, what seems to be troubling you?"

The sister in question hefted her chin. "I'm not your *dearest*, and we all know it."

"You are all equally dear to me." Kate spoke so quietly that her words might've gotten lost in the clatter of the coach wheels.

Even in the dim coach's interior, Kate could see her sister puffing up like an adder ready to strike. She waited patiently, knowing from experience it would not be long before Sadie spoke her mind.

Only a few seconds passed before Sadie straightened in her seat, bristling like a chipmunk robbed of her acorn. "Very well! If you really want to know, I shall tell you. Why should I be relegated to tending the sick and wounded here in this miserable coach? Hhmm?"

Miserable? Aunt Honore's coach was luxurious by any standard. Kate merely shrugged. "I don't know, dear. Why should you?"

"Precisely the point. It should've been Nora stuck in here, not me. Nora is better suited for this sort of thing—" She gesticulated wildly in Kate and Lord Colter's direction. "Tending to people's wounds and seeing that they don't choke in their sleep. But oh, no. Because of you, I am no longer our aunt's favorite."

"You're not?" Kate blinked at her sister's exuberant complaints.

"No!" Sadie snapped. "And why, you might ask, does Lady Alameda prefer Nora's company over mine when everyone knows Nora is as dull as an old stick, whereas I would've had a rollicking good time in Lord Weathervane's fine coach? And we all know Nora will sit there the whole way with her hands folded as prim and stiff as a nun on Sunday." Sadie finally paused long enough for a breath. "And it's all because of you! You caused too much of a fuss at the inn and gave Lady Alameda a headache. Now, she says Nora is the only one of us who knows how to be silent. That's why!"

"Nora is not dull." Kate leaned back against Lady Alameda's plush seat.

"Not in the least." Greyson rumbled in agreement. "Your sister is a fine gentle-hearted girl. Too good and too sweet-natured to be exposed to that scoundrel Weatherford." He spoke all this from the depths of his corner, his eyes closed as if resting.

Kate's attention snapped to him. It had been his tone that snagged her notice so completely—the depth of sincerity and respect with which he defended her sister. It touched her, but at the same time, it aroused a strange sensation in her bosom akin to . . . to . . .

Jealousy?

Preposterous! It couldn't be.

And yet there it was—a glowing green-eyed serpent crawling through the night, chomping at her heart.

No, *no, no,* she brushed it aside.

What did she care if Greyson thought highly of her sister and lowly of her? Nora deserved praise. She was a modest, angelic, charming young lady. It would only be natural for Lord Colter to admire her. Unlike Kate, Nora was the very pattern-card of how a young lady ought to behave. Not to mention, she was phenomenally beautiful.

Everyone admired Nora.

Kate folded her hands together and squared her shoulders. She didn't have a jealous bone in her body. The whole idea was absurd. Aunt Honore must've spiked her tea with some foul breed of laudanum. In fact, now that she considered it, Nora would be the exact right sort of girl for Lord Colter. He said it himself: Nora is genteel and sweet-natured. They were perfect for one another.

Ideal.

Kate's stomach felt unaccountably nauseous. It must be aftereffects from the laudanum—or the bumpiness of the road, or the humdrum clacking of wheels and hooves. Maybe it was the stuffiness of the carriage or that incessant buzzing of insects outside.

It could be anything causing this uncomfortable feeling. *Anything* except jealousy.

She would never have any such feelings toward Nora, the dearest, sweetest, most innocent—

Oh no . . .

Kate remembered her duty in life.

Concern for Nora's welfare rose like a sudden, fierce storm. She, Sadie, and Tilly sat in their comfortable carriage under the safety and protection of Lord Colter when at this very moment, Nora might be subjected to their capricious aunt's neglect and the advances of that rascal, Lord Weatherford.

"Nora!" She sat bolt upright. "We've got to do something!"

Her outburst startled all of them. Sadie nodded and scooted closer. "Yes. That's what I was saying. It should be me rather than Nora."

"No! No. Don't you see? Aunt Honore can't be trusted to properly chaperone you or her or anyone. Nora should be here with us, not in Lord Weatherford's carriage."

Tilly clucked her tongue. "I think you mean in Lord Wetfoot's carriage."

"I mean we have to stop. Now! We must turn the coach around and rescue her from them."

"I hardly think *she* needs rescuing. I'm the one who needs to be rescued." Sadie slumped back against the seat. "Besides, turning around won't do a bit of good; they're bound to be miles ahead of us."

"True." Tilly always sided with Sadie. "His coach sprang out of the courtyard a good fifteen minutes ahead of ours, and his vehicle is much lighter. Even if we were about to catch up to them, where would Nora sit? Aunt Honore said there wasn't room for Nora in our coach, given Lord Colter's gargantuan size."

"I am not gargantuan," he rumbled with irritation.

"*You* understand my concern, don't you, my lord?" Kate almost reached for him in her appeal, but pulled her hand back just in time.

"Well, er . . ." He fixed his gaze too closely upon the progress of her hand. "Yes. I suppose so. Although, given these particular circumstances—"

"*These circumstances?*" Sadie huffed loudly. "You mean Nora enjoying our aunt's witty conversation and Lord Weatherford's jests—those circumstances?"

"Don't be naïve. She's a complete innocent, and he's a rake of the first order." Kate blinked at Sadie's callous disregard for their sister's welfare. "She's my younger sister, and—"

"Fiddlesticks." Sadie swatted the air and kicked her foot out, narrowly missing Kate's shin. "She's my sister, too, and you obviously don't know her as well as I do. Nora is far from naïve."

"I do so."

"And I can prove it." Sadie warmed to her subject, leaning forward with such heat she practically glowed red, even in the dark. "You're always too busy ordering us around to really know her. Nora never gets angry or flustered the way you do. *She* can always be relied upon to keep a sensible head on her shoulders."

Sadie's words stung worse than a slap. Kate didn't know how to answer.

"It's true." Tilly leaned in, nodding. "Nora is almost always sensible. For instance, she warned us not to try to feed your letter to Ralphie."

"And yet, you did it anyway. I would've stopped the two of you." Kate leaned closely enough to make sure her triumphant glare was visible to her ungrateful siblings. "Lord Colter, kindly tell my sisters exactly how reasonable I am." He hesitated, and so she added, "Oh, I'm willing to admit I may lose my temper now and then, but I am always sensible!"

Tilly giggled.

She actually giggled out loud. And unless Kate was mistaken, that was a sardonic snort emanating from Greyson's side of the coach. She whipped around to scowl at him. "Tell them!"

He instantly sobered. "Kate, dearest, I, uh . . . well, yes. Yes, you are extremely capable and often wise—"

Tilly stopped snickering and interrupted, "Surely you can see he is merely trying to appease you, Katie. If you were so very sensible, we wouldn't be here in this coach, would we? We'd be at home with Papa, and I would be able to go outside and play with Ralphie, and you—"

"You asked to come along on this trip," Kate snapped. "And children should speak when spoken to, and not one solitary minute before." Kate hated that every word Tilly said was true. Gall soured her throat. "Do you hear me, young lady?"

"But—"

"No buts."

Sadie exhaled derisively. "I don't see how you can call her a child and a young lady all in one breath."

"That will be enough out of you, too, missy." She pressed her hands against the leather seats. "Now, I will see what can be done about Nora." She faced Greyson squarely. "How far ahead of us do you reckon they are?"

He tilted his head speculatively. "Given his team and equipage, a mile or two."

"Very well, a mile can be made up if we've a mind to do so." Kate stumbled to her feet, wobbling from side to side as the coach rumbled over another dip in the road. She knocked on the small sliding panel above her sisters' heads. "Driver! Oh, I say, driver!"

No response.

Sadie sniffed arrogantly. "He's probably half-asleep. I would be, too, given the monotony of this road at night."

Kate heartily wished Sadie *were* asleep. "Feel free to nap, dearest." She tried to keep the sarcasm out of her voice.

She knelt on the seat and struggled with the small panel until she finally got it to slide halfway. "Driver," she called again. "Mr. Coachman? Sir?" For all her trouble, she was rewarded with a face full of wind and a gnat in her mouth. She sputtered and brushed it aside.

Lord Colter rumbled as if he thought it was funny to watch her struggle. She ignored him and banged her hand against the roof. All to no avail. Forcing the useless portal shut, she glanced around the interior of the coach and went for bigger game. The window.

She lowered the window glass and stuck her head out. It was awfully dark out there and rather windy. She hadn't realized how windy until it whipped her hair to tatters. Over the horses' clattering hoofs and jangling harnesses, she heard Greyson call out behind her. "Kate! What are you doing?" He sounded openly annoyed.

"Rescuing my sister, of course." And rescue Nora she would. The wind, the wheels, and the horses beat against her ears much more loudly than she anticipated. "Driver!" she shouted. "Oye, coachman!" Maybe Sadie was right and the fellow was half-asleep. Kate pushed herself farther through the window until her hips rested on the sill.

"For pity's sake, Kate. Get down from there!" Was that alarm thundering from Lord Colter? Or anger?

What did it matter? She could barely hear him anyway. Kate raised her fist to pound on the side of the coach. Surely *that* would awaken the driver. At that inopportune moment, the wheel nearest her clunked over a sizeable boulder.

Up she bounced. Her body twisted awkwardly. Her arms flew wide. She recovered and reached for something to cling to—*anything.*

Found nothing.

Nothing but night air.

She was falling. Kate emitted a very unladylike sound. Something akin to, "Oohheeaaaii!"

Despite only moonlight, she spied far more of the gravel road than she cared to see, and she was headed straight for it.

_Chapter 10
Rescued From Ruin

TIME SEEMED TO STOP. In less than a blink, Kate's mind conjured her demise. *Limbs crushed beneath the wheels, her cheeks and nose torn to shreds, blood pooling in the grit and grime of the road.*

But . . .

Instead of the mouthful of rocks and gravel she expected, her descent halted. A strong arm from inside the coach clasped her roughly and pulled her to safety. Two smaller hands tugged at each of her ankles.

Kate collapsed in an undignified heap onto the safety of the coach floor. Blinking up at them, she remembered her manners and smiled. "Thank you."

They did not look pleased.

Especially Lord Colter. Kate had seen angry bulls wearing more pleasant expressions. Even Sadie looked miffed—she crossed her arms and rudely turned her gaze up to the ceiling.

Tilly stared hard at Kate. "You could've been killed. Trampled under the wheels." Worry pinched up her sweet little face and, *oh dear*, her eyes were watering. "You could've been killed, Katie. *Killed dead!*"

Kate opened her mouth to protest, or to explain that if one were *killed*, obviously one would already be dead. And also, that it was impossible to be *trampled* by wheels, but rather one would be *crushed* by them. Except it didn't seem the appropriate time. Added to that, Kate recollected, all too keenly, exactly how close she'd come to sampling the gravel with her teeth.

In lieu of correcting her little sister, Kate did her best to straighten her traveling pelisse. Then, with as much dignity as she could muster, she struggled to get up from the floor. Lord Colter offered her a hand, but she preferred not to accept his bad-tempered aid and hoisted herself up, plopping unceremoniously onto an open seat.

Her jaunt out the window had caused them all to shift positions. Lord Colter, glowering rather heavily, took the seat straight across from her. "What in blazes were you trying to accomplish with that stunt?"

"I think it is perfectly obvious." She stared unflinchingly into their disapproving faces. "I was trying to save my sister. *Our* sister." She emphasized pointedly to Sadie and Tilly. When they continued to scowl at her, she brushed out her skirts. "And I must say, given how oblivious the coachman was to my efforts to gain his attention, it is quite possible he really *has* fallen asleep. We may all be in danger, as well."

None of them rose to the bait.

"Is there something you would like me to help you with?" Greyson took the annoying tone of an adult patiently talking to a small pudding-headed child.

And Kate did not like it.

Not one bit.

She sniffed. "I want the ruddy coachman to speed up," she snapped. "Run the horses. He has six of them, after all. There is no reason why he can't. We need to catch up to Lord Weatherford's carriage before it is too late."

"You mean Lord Weather*fib*'s carriage." Tilly seemed to have lost some of her enthusiasm for nicknaming the lord in question.

Kate exhaled her irritation. "I do not care what you call that wretched oaf—we have to catch them."

Lord Colter drummed his fingers on his thigh impatiently. "Why is it you will never ask for help?"

"Begging your pardon?" She did her best to pretend she did not grasp his meaning. At his condemning silence, she shrugged. "I did ask."

"You did not."

"Well, I made my intentions clear."

"You did not ask." Greyson stood, his hand clenched in a tight fist, but instead of throttling her as she fleetingly feared he might do, he rapped soundly on the ceiling.

The little panel above her head magically slid open, and the coachman bellowed in at them, "Yes, m'lord?"

Greyson answered, "Make haste, my good man. We need overtake Lord Weatherford's carriage. It is of the utmost importance."

"Aye, m'lord." The coachman's whip cracked, and the fellow

whistled loud enough to awaken the dead. Their coach lurched forward.

It had been so easily done. Kate intended to lower her chin and close her mouth; instead, it bobbled aimlessly until she managed to protest her disbelief. "I did that very thing—I knocked."

He clasped her wrist and extended his other hand to her, balling it into a fist. "Your hand. My hand. Which do you think makes a more noticeable thump?"

She tugged free of his massive paw, refusing to dignify his cross behavior with an answer. His impatience stung. He would not treat Nora this way.

He hovered over her, his ire nearly searing a hole in her forehead. "Most people would simply say thank you."

"Would they?" She sniffed. "I wonder."

The coach's galloping pace rattled her teeth. With a bone-jarring thunk, the front wheels bumped over something in the road. The vehicle launched itself into the air, bouncing Kate and her sisters up from their seats. Apart from Tilly's surprised grunt, everything went soundless for a moment—no more crunching or rattling or grinding beneath the wheels.

An instant later, they landed with a jolting thud. Springs squawked. The coach tilted wildly, first one way and then the other. Lord Colter slammed against the door jamb, winced, and fell back against the seat, clutching his injured shoulder.

"You're hurt!" She scrambled up.

"Sit down," he barked at her. "I'll be fine."

Kate slowly withdrew her hand and lowered herself back into the seat. She thought she spotted a tinge of fresh blood on his shirt, but clearly, he did not want her help. Racing along with the moonlight shining through the open window, she couldn't help but notice how like a wounded boy he looked. His cheeks were flushed, and his hair was so tousled her fingers itched to comb through it. And he kept vexing the corner of his lip, as if gnawing on it might summon a solution to his problem.

His angst made her feel . . . sad?

No, it was more than that—she felt . . . *sorry*. Sorry she had caused him pain. Truth stuck its cruel knee in her stomach and made her curl up uncomfortably.

Fifteen minutes later, the inscrutable coachman's portal slid open again. "Coming up on 'em now, m'lord. Not more'n a furlong away."

"Well done! Thank you." Greyson's voice reflected none of the boyish hurt she'd observed a few seconds earlier. It resonated with authority—low, full-grown manliness. Rock steady and in charge. Kate swallowed, except her throat felt dry, probably from the dust of the road, and her cheeks burned. She was not blushing. What did she have to blush about? She touched two of her gloved fingers against her cheek, testing for heat, staring in his direction. Beneath those slender rays of moonlight, she wondered if she might be seeing him clearly for the very first time.

Their driver blew a horn and shouted a halloo. The coach slowed and pulled to a stop beside Lord Weatherford's vehicle. Kate lurched from her seat, not waiting for the coachman to climb down and lower the steps.

Anyway, he was too busy answering the other driver's question; "What's a do?"

She jumped down, her traveling boots crunching against the

gravel as she marched straight toward that rascal Weatherford's carriage door. With each step, she formulated a scathing peal to ring over his head and over Aunt Honore's head—over all of their heads.

She paused near the polished black door and heard the sound of laughter emanating from the interior—Nora's and a gentleman's. Visions of seduction ran screaming through the hallways of her mind. She was just about to rip the door from its hinges when it swung open.

"Oh! It's you. I had wondered why we'd stopped." Lord Weatherford smiled pleasantly at Kate, *the cheeky rogue!* As if he hadn't just been caught in the act of seducing her younger sister.

She shoved him back in his seat and leaned into the interior.

All three of them smiled at her, not showing the least bit of embarrassment by their behavior. The interior lanterns flickered gaily.

Kate squinted at them. Nora appeared fully clothed and not a hair out of place. Lord Weatherford smiled pleasantly as if he had just been enjoying listening to a lively story. Aunt Honore sat between the two. She stopped smiling and lifted a lorgnette to peer at Kate. "What the devil happened to you?"

Kate had forgotten about her disheveled hair and her rumpled frock. She had been wearing a proper bonnet at one time, but could not recollect at what point she'd lost it. It must've fallen off sometime before slobbering all over Lord Colter. She ignored her devious aunt and addressed her sister. "Nora, are you all right?"

"Yes, thank you," Nora said, as if they'd just happened upon one another on the village street. "Indeed, I'm quite comfortable.

But, Katie, dearest, are you well? You look a trifle, um, frayed—"

"*Frayed.* Ha!" Aunt Honore snorted. "Looks as if you've been wrestling with a hedgehog."

A *hedgehog?*

"A hedgehog is a small—oh, never mind!" Kate tensed so hard her spine nearly snapped. "My present condition is thanks to you and your laudanum!"

"Humph. Thought I gave you enough to get us to London." Aunt Honore shrugged. "Your nerves were overset. I had to do something."

"My nerves were in perfect order. More importantly, my sister should not be in this vehicle. It isn't proper. She must ride in the coach with us. Come, Nora."

"Must she?" Lord Weatherford scooted forward, blocking the way. "I don't know when I've enjoyed anyone's company as much as I have hers."

"I'm quite safe riding with them, Katie. Lord Weather—" At a nudge and glare from their aunt, Nora swallowed back his name. "Lord Weathermarch is behaving like a perfect gentleman."

"It's true! I *am* behaving." Lord Weatherford beamed and puffed out his chest, ridiculously proud of himself.

A silly gesture. Yet he seemed genuinely sincere. Kate frowned, unable to fathom any kind of earnest sentiment from this scoundrel.

He patted her hand as she gripped the doorway. "I don't blame you for doubting me. I can scarcely believe it myself. It's a marvel, Miss Linnet. What can I say? Your sister puts me on my best behavior. I've no idea why, unless it is simply because she is the loveliest, gentlest, sweetest creature in all of heaven or—"

"Stop, Neddy. Stop! I beg you." Aunt Honore clasped his forearm. "You're waxing poetic. I won't have it. It simply won't do. Truth be told, coming from you, it frightens me."

"Hhmm." He eased back a bit, blinking. "Frightens me, too, now that you mention it." He turned to gaze at Nora. "Perhaps it's because I'm unaccustomed to such angelic charm."

Charm? Nora?

"—her innocence and depth of sincerity." Lord Weatherford continued rhapsodizing and complimenting her sister as if the poor child wasn't sitting right there, blushing down to her saintly toes. He shook his head as if trying to escape her spell. "It is as if she truly cares for the people around her. For instance, *you*, Miss Linnet. You should hear how glowingly she speaks of your character, how lovingly she recounts your many escapades."

My many escapades?

One of Kate's eyes twitched crazily. "Nevertheless, my lord, I must insist that my sister travel with us."

Lord Weatherford's countenance fell. "I beg you to reconsider. I shall be grieved to part with her. Think of how her presence is mending my character."

Kate exhaled her frustration. "I'm afraid mending your character is none of my concern—"

"Now who's being a bad Samaritan?" Aunt Honore snickered at her.

"This is different." Kate pointed to the gravel beside her. "Come along, Nora."

Lord Weatherford leaned forward to protest again, but Lord Colter's commanding voice boomed out from behind her. "You'd best do as the young lady asks. Aside from that, Weatherford, your character is beyond repair."

Until then, Kate hadn't realized Greyson, Tilly, and Sadie stood behind her. His strength flowed around her, like a magical cushion of support. She stepped back, basking in his nearness.

"Don't be a grudge," Lord Weatherford grumbled. "I could change."

Nora, in her annoyingly soft, melodic voice, added, "It's true, my lord. No one is beyond redemption."

"I suspect he is." Lord Colter pushed closer. "Be sensible, Neddy. It's dangerous to leave the horses standing out here in the dark. We're blocking the road on both sides. If another coach comes along, they'll be hard pressed to pull up in time."

As if hearing their mention, one of Lord Weatherford's team snorted, stamped his hoof, and shook his harness. Nora pushed gently past Lord Weatherford and climbed down into Kate's arms. "I never intended to distress you."

"Never mind." Kate clasped her sister around the waist and hurried her to the waiting coach. "Let's be on our way before we cause a collision here on the highway."

Lord Colter handed them up into the vehicle and quietly confided, "This time of night, it's unlikely that there would be any other travelers."

"But you said—"

"Merely coming to your aid, my dear." His hand remained on Kate's waist a little longer than necessary, and his husky words melted into her ears.

She drew in a quick breath. "You needn't have done so. I had the situation well in hand."

"Of course you did." He gruffed loudly. "Never doubted it for a minute."

Squished as they now were on the seats, his grumpy attitude set the tone for the ride to London. Sadie sulked in the shadows. Tilly fell into a fitful slumber on Nora's shoulder. He, *the one who started it all*, leaned back and feigned sleep. She could tell it was a pretense by the frown darkening his features. Not that Kate was looking too closely. She wasn't. Although her head throbbed abominably, and she reluctantly admitted to herself that she would very much like to rest it on his comfortable chest. So much so that she considered, *perhaps*, making an apology, *of sorts*. Except he seemed so very annoyed with her that she couldn't bring herself to do it. Although why he should be annoyed with her to such a degree escaped her.

Out of the blue, to no one in particular, Kate announced, "I *do* ask for help." The words spilled out, unbidden. Maybe because his earlier accusation kept rolling round and round like a demented croquet ball, banging mercilessly against the walls of her skull. "I do!" she said louder.

He snorted.

Nora sighed with saintly delicacy.

And Sadie simply said, "Balderdash."

_Chapter 11
Pickling the Perfect Plan

K ATE PONDERED HER predicament until it could be prodded and kneaded no more. She finally gave up and fell into an exhausted sleep. The coach lurched to a stop and the door opened to its blinking occupants. Aunt Honore stood in front of a building that looked more like a Greek temple than a townhouse. "Don't just sit there like lumps. Climb out. We're here! Welcome to Alison Hall. Hurry up now, and don't keep the servants standing. It's the middle of the night, and I wish to be in my bed before the sun rises."

"I've read Lord Byron's book about vampires," Tilly mumbled sleepily as she climbed down. "Do you think our aunt is—"

"No." Kate clamped a firm hand on her little sister's shoulder. "No, I don't. And it would be best if you kept such thoughts to yourself."

Lord Colter stepped down behind them, but remained beside the coach. "Lady Alameda, you've been most accommodating, and I owe you a debt of gratitude. However, given the late hour, I wonder if you could spare your driver for a few minutes longer so that he might drive me to my rooms? They are but a few blocks away on Piccadilly."

"What?" Kate's hands flew up as if to catch herself from falling—except she hadn't stumbled at all. "No, you mustn't!" She spun on her heel. "Surely you will stay the night with us. Your wound needs to be tended, the dressings changed, and—"

He shook his head. "I cannot impose on Lady Alameda's hospitality any longer than I already have."

"Oh, but she doesn't mind. Do you, Aunt? You cannot take care of your arm properly, not without help."

"Kate, stop." He took a step toward her and that seem-ed to steady her a bit, but his words did not. "I am a grown man. I will manage."

She tried to shake off his answer. "Do be reasonable, my lord. You cannot possibly change the bandage yourself. Aunt Honore, tell him he can't go."

Honore grumbled rather loudly and Kate could almost hear her aunt's eyes rolling up to the starless night sky. "You heard him, Kate. He's a grown man. Who am I to tell him what he can or cannot do?" She turned sharply to the coachman. "John, as soon as the servants have removed our luggage, kindly take Lord Colter to his lodgings."

With a perturbed sniff, Aunt Honore turned and marched up the stairs. "Come along, Kate. And don't be difficult, or I swear I shall pour more laudanum down your throat, even if I have to sit on you to do it."

Kate stood frozen on the walk, staring up at him. "You're going . . . a-away?" She didn't mean to sound like such a pitiful child.

"Yes." He studied her face as if trying to decipher her thoughts. "Isn't that what you wanted—to be rid of me?"

She swallowed the thorny lump rising in her throat. "No, it was you who wanted to be rid of me. You made yourself abundantly clear at the ball." Why, oh why, were her words shaking as if she might burst into tears? She was not the crying sort.

He tilted his head, studying her crumbling features too intently. "Well . . . now I don't. And you know it." He took another step, closing the distance between them, unnerving her completely. His voice flowed over her, low and steady, unrelenting in its warmth. "We are here only because you refused to get re-engaged to me."

It was true.

Only now . . . the thought of being away from him, of not having him just down the road, or the idea that he wouldn't be calling on her every day—it was . . . it was unsettling. She made a soft mewing sound, like a silly lost kitten.

Be brave, Kate.

She lowered her eyes, unable to look at him, afraid he would read her distress. She caught her bottom lip to keep her mouth quiet. Part of her wanted to beg him not to go. Another part wanted to run away and sob her miserable, confused self to sleep. Her leg jiggled nervously.

Still staring at the toes of his boots, she mumbled, "Will you call on us?"

Us?

She said it as if she had meant her entire family, not merely herself. And Kate hated herself for being a coward.

"If you would like me to?"

She felt him leaning down to hear her reply. His nearness wrapped around her like a favorite quilt. She wanted to look up, except if she did, she might do something stupid out of desperation, such as fall into his arms and kiss him. Not an appropriate response to the situation.

Not at all.

She managed a childish nod and tore away from him, dashing up the stairs, hoping he wouldn't see her face turning red in the dim light. At the top, she dared to check over her shoulder. Lord Colter stared after her with a most puzzling look on his face.

Aunt Honore yanked Kate inside the doorway. "If you are quite through torturing that young man, I will show you and your sisters to your rooms."

The door closed, and Kate mutely followed her aunt up an ornate marble staircase. Their rooms were far more spacious than the bedroom they shared at home. Sadie and Nora disappeared into an adjoining suite, which they would share. Kate thanked her aunt, who gave her a weary "humph" and left them to their own devices.

Kate dismissed the maid, insisting that she could unpack for herself in the morning. Tilly quickly changed into her nightrail and crawled into the enormous bed they would share. Kate silently tucked in her sleepy little sister, smoothing back the child's fair curls, but all the while she kept seeing that odd expression on Greyson's face.

Night closed in around Kate, wrapping her in a profound aloneness. She wandered through the bedroom like a lost sleepwalking ghost. She failed to locate her nightclothes and decided it didn't matter.

Disrobing down to her chemise, she left her traveling gown in a heap on the floor and climbed into bed. But she'd forgotten to extinguish the oil lamp on the bed table and it flickered annoyingly. With a heavy sigh, she sat up and turned down the wick, drowning the flame. She sat there listlessly, watching the smoke drift up through the dark like the tangled yarn of her mind.

Lord Colter was gone.

Vanished like the slender threads of smoke.

Would he come back? He said he would call—if she wanted him to—and that meant he would, *wouldn't he?*

Curse her slow-witted tongue—if only she'd done more than nod.

He understood she wanted him to call, didn't he? The more she thought about it, the surer she felt. And if he did come calling, she needed to have a plan.

But . . .

A plan to do what?

Kate flopped back against the pillow and stared at the dark ceiling. She wanted to keep him in her life. His friendship meant more to her than she'd realized. How could she keep him in her circle? Well, firstly, she needed to convince him, *somehow*, that she could be as sweet and charming and *un-henpeck-y* as Nora. Yes, that was of paramount importance. She needed to be more likeable.

But how?

Hhmm.

The solution seemed simple enough. All she needed to do was stop ordering everyone about. She could do that. *Child's play.* She pulled the covers up under her chin.

In fact, I'll be so sweet and charming that all of London will fall at my feet and then . . . then what?

Visions of lovesick suitors lined up outside Aunt Honore's Greek temple of a townhouse danced in her head. She pictured Lord Colter fighting his way through the crowd and kneeling at her feet, begging her to reconsider his offer, promising to never again lose his patience with her.

It was a pretty dream.

Very pretty.

Too bad morning came so glaringly bright and brought those dreams crashing down around her ears.

Chapter 12
London Visions Falling Down

"WAKE UP."

"Katie!" *Someone*, namely Tilly, rudely jostled her shoulder. "Kaaatieee. You have to wake up."

"It's too early," Kate grumbled, tossing to her other side and covering her head with the pillow. "Go back to sleep, Tilly."

Tilly lifted the corner of the pillow and invaded Kate's inner sanctum of sleep. "But Katie," she whispered, "it isn't early. It's 2:30 in the afternoon, and I've been up for hours. More importantly, Lord Weatherbottom is here to see Nora. He brought her the most enormous bouquet of flowers I have ever seen!" Tilly wriggled so close her breath tickled Kate's nose. "And that's not all. He gave her a box of tiny little cakes. I ate one and it was divine. He even brought a bottle of French wine for Aunt Honore. He keeps asking if he might speak to you, but Aunt Honore told him no, that we should not waken a sleeping tiger.

But he says it is a matter of grave importance, and that he cannot possibly wait."

Tilly stopped yammering and poked her finger in Kate's ear. "Did you hear me, Katie? I think he means to ask you for permission to court Nora."

"What!?" Kate yanked the pillow off of her head and sat up. "What did you say?"

Tilly harrumphed the same exact way Aunt Honore does. "You heard me. He's acting like a lovesick donkey."

"Monkey," Kate corrected and tried to rub the sleep out of her eyes.

"I said donkey because I was trying not to say jackass. But if you prefer—"

"No. No, donkey is fine."

Tilly stood atop the mattress and peered sternly down at Kate. "I don't think you understand. He won't stop staring at Nora, even though Aunt Honore told him to mind his manners and start behaving like a grown man instead of an idiot schoolboy." Tilly gestured broadly with her hands. "He didn't even get mad about that. He just sighed and kept smiling so stupidly that it makes me wonder if something in his head is broken." Tilly began jiggling up and down as if testing the mattress ticking. "Sadie thinks it is all vastly entertaining and she refuses to do a thing about it. You have to come down and straighten things out. Now!"

Kate felt as if she had an anvil teetering atop her head and her mouth was stuffed with cotton wadding. No doubt, the aftereffects of laudanum. She blinked groggily at Tilly, who kept bobbling all over the bed. "For pity's sake, Tilly, hold still."

"Are you coming down or not?" In her agitated state, Tilly

did not refrain from bouncing. "If you won't come down, I shall tell him to go away and never come back. I doubt he will listen to me, but at least I will try."

"You will do nothing of the sort. Proper young ladies do not issue such demanding statements to gentleman callers."

"You do. Or you *would*, if you'd get up and go down-stairs."

"I would not."

Or at least, not anymore.

"And young ladies do not bounce on beds, either. You are in London now, and . . ." Kate was too parched to con-tinue. "Hand me a glass of water, will you?"

"Why are you in your underclothes?" Tilly leapt off the bed and poured a glass of lemon water from a pitcher. "You told me I must always wear my nightgown so I would be modestly clad in case of a fire. Don't you care about your own modesty?"

Kate gulped down the lemon water and decided to ignore Tilly's question. "I will get dressed as soon as I can and come down to assess for myself the situation with Lord Weatherford."

Tilly studied Kate for a moment before her mouth twitched sideways. "Umm, you're going to need help. Your hair looks like you got trampled at the opera."

Kate reached up and felt the tangles encircling her head. "Don't be ridiculous. You know perfectly well I was not at an opera last night. And anyway, one does not get trampled at the opera."

"One might, if one is at the opera house and fire breaks out, and who knows what else might happen at one of those places." Tilly stopped her infernal bounding around, planted her fists on her hips, and narrowed a frown at Kate. "And that addlepated Lord Weatherdrizzle has asked permission to take our Nora to the opera."

"The *opera*? She can't! She's too young for such things. She'll never fend him off in one of those dark, private boxes. Did Aunt Honore tell him no? Of course not. One cannot rely upon her to do anything sensible. Never mind. I will put a stop to this. You find a brush. I'll put on a morning gown."

Ten minutes later, Kate emerged fully clothed—albeit in a wrinkled dress and mismatched stockings, but at least she wasn't naked, and her hair no longer resembled an unruly lion's mane. It didn't matter that Tilly had yanked out several handfuls while taming it.

"Which way?" Kate demanded, wishing the white, curv-ing walls and all the Greek goddesses carved into them did not make her feel quite so dizzy.

Tilly crooked her finger and scampered ahead of her. "Follow me."

Kate held the rail as they rushed down a wide, alabaster staircase that curled around four stories to a sitting room on the first floor.

"Nora!" Kate barked, bursting into the room ready to rescue her helpless cub of a sister and finding it inhabited—not by *one* disreputable male as she'd expected, but by a half dozen or more gentlemen.

Suitors.

Kate could tell by their meticulously tied cravats, their artistically combed hair, their gleaming buckle shoes, and their preening stances. *But why?* Why were they here? And why this great a number? So many gentlemen and flower arrangements littered the sitting room that it was difficult to ascertain a headcount.

Small, tasteful bouquets were strewn on side tables and the fireplace mantle, but on the tea table in front of the large sofa sat a massive arrangement of roses, lilies, and bright yellow flowers. The overpowering scent made Kate's nose itch.

She took a step backward, regretting she hadn't taken more care with her appearance, wishing they weren't all staring at her. These were obviously gentlemen of the highest rank and Kate stood in their midst dressed like a farmgirl on wash day. Her throat, which was already dry, withered as if she'd swallowed ashes. This was no way to begin her assault on London high society.

Turn and run!

Before she could obey her inner dictum, Lord Weatherwhistle sprang up as if he'd spotted the queen. "There you are, Miss Linnet. Finally! I've been waiting all morning for an audience with you. Might I have a private word?"

"Here?" Kate managed to gasp. It seemed as if every eye in the room was trained on her, leaning in to hear her answer. "I-I . . ."

Aunt Honore stood and brushed out her skirts, not that hers were wrinkled. "I tried to tell him you were indisposed today."

"Nonsense!" Lord Weatherweasel argued. "She looks hale and hearty enough. Why, I've seen milkmaids less sturdy." He patted her shoulder as if they were old friends.

"Isn't that so?" He squinted, taking a harder look. "Well, hhmm. Admittedly, she might look a bit white around the gills, but nothing a little biscuit and some tea won't cure. Isn't that so?" When she didn't answer, he backed up a step. "Er . . . you do know, don't you, my dear, that you've one pink stocking on your left foot and a lavender one on the right?"

Kate experienced a split second of gratitude that she did not have a loaded pistol in her hand, for she most certainly would've shot him. As it was, both hands balled into tight fists and her right foot arched with an intense desire to kick his left kneecap across the room. "My stockings should be of no concern to you, sirrah."

At that, he backed up in alarm. "I meant no disrespect, Miss Linnet. Quite the opposite. Your well-being is of primary importance to me, for I hope to be closely connected with you in the future." He glanced over his shoulder, grinning broadly at Nora, who sat barely visible behind the roses and lilies.

Kate glared at him. "Such talk is woefully premature, my lord."

Aunt Honore let out an enormous sigh. "I tried to tell him as much. He simply will not listen to reason."

At that moment, Lady Alameda's elderly butler stepped into the doorway. "M'lady, pardon the intrusion. Lady Jersey has arrived. Are you at home?"

Lady Jersey?

The *Lady Jersey?*

Surely not. Suddenly dizzy, Kate reached for a side table to support herself.

Before Aunt Honore could answer, a grand lady swept through the doorway. "Don't be a fussy-duck, Cairn. She is *always* at home to me." The lady bustled forward and took in the surroundings, the numerous gentlemen strewn about the room, and the flowers crowding every surface. She paused, briefly glancing down her nose at Kate, and leaned forward to kiss each of Honore's cheeks as do the French aristocracy.

Honore laughed gaily. "Lady Jersey, what an unexpected surprise."

It is Lady Jersey.

The most illustrious of the patronesses of Almack's. Admission through the hallowed doors of Almack's social club required a voucher card, and those coveted cards had to be signed, sealed, and issued by one of the seven lady patronesses of Almack's.

Kate stepped back, bumping against the side table, pulling Tilly in front of her to hide her shabby ensemble.

If only she had dressed with more care.

Any young lady hoping for an advantageous marriage might wait weeks, or even months, for an audience with one of these formidable patronesses. In point of fact, one might never be granted an audience at all. Yet to Kate's utter astonishment, and embarrassment, Lady Jersey stood right here in her aunt's drawing room.

If only the great lady hadn't come today of all days, when Kate looked such a rumpled frumpkin. Kate contemplated crawling under the thick Turkish rug to hide. On the other hand, maybe she was still dreaming, trapped in a horrid laudanum-driven nightmare. She pinched her arm. Hard.

Nope.

Still here.

Lady Jersey tugged her train and swirled it around her majestically as if she were posing for a painting. "My dear Honore, your receiving room seems to be grooooossly overcrooowded." She elongated all of her vowels in a most dramatic and superior manner. Turning to the gawking occupants, she gestured with her closed fan at one of the gentlemen fawning over Nora. "You there! Yes, you, young Tarleton. Take yourself off. You've been here long enough. Go. And take your friends with you."

All the gentlemen in the room stared at her open-mouthed.

When they didn't immediately dash for the door, she raised her voice. "Youuu heard me. Be gooone! I wish to have a private conversation with Lady Alameda."

Lady Alameda stood with barely contained mirth, watching her guests stumble and bow their way out the door.

Lady Jersey turned and arched a brow sternly at Lord Weatherford. "That goes for you, too, Lord Weeatherfiioooouard." She seemed to incorporate every vowel possible into his name. "Run along." She flicked her fingers at him.

Grinning broadly at their new arrival, Tilly tugged on Kate's hand and whispered, "I liiiike heeer."

Kate pinched her little sister for mimicking Lady Jersey's accent and turned to her aunt. "We shall leave as well and give you your privacy. Come along, Tilly." She waved to Nora and Sadie.

"Noooooo, my dear. Youuew will stay."

Oh dear. This did not bode well for Kate's future.

Aunt Honore's drawing room seemed surprisingly spacious, now that it wasn't cluttered with gentlemen callers. Lady Alameda guided Lady Jersey to the oversized sofa in the center of the room, the one Nora had just vacated, and offered her guest the seat of honor.

Aunt Honor sat herself in a throne-like carved chair. "Now then, to what do we owe the pleasure of your company?"

"Is this the gel?" Lady Jersey nodded skeptically in Kate's direction and sniffed haughtily. "I find it difficult to believe *she* could've brought Weatherford to heel. Look at her, Honore. Her gown is in need of an iron and her hair looks as if a four-year-old pinned it up."

"I'm ten," Tilly protested. "We were in a hurry."

"Hush." Kate said through gritted teeth. She stood behind Tilly's chair, trying to hide her ankles by crossing one foot in front of the other without falling over.

Honore rolled her eyes to the ceiling before pasting on a smile. "Lady Jersey, allow me the dubious honor of presenting my nieces. Miss Linnet, the one you see bobbling awkwardly, is the eldest of the four. And this creature next to you is her sister, Miss Nora Linnet. It is she who has captivated Lord Weatherford's attention—although I'm certain it will prove to be merely a passing fancy."

"I wonder." Lady Jersey arched one brow imperiously. "Seems the young buck has been trotting all about town declaring his undying love for your incomparable niece. All of Mayfair is buzzing with the news."

"Waxing poetic, was he?" Honore sniffed irritably. "I warned the young jackanapes to stop spouting such nonsense."

"Never known him to be the sort who listens to wisdom." Lady Jersey gestured at Tilly and Sadie. "And these other children?"

Honore grumbled. "Meet trouble one and trouble two. Sadie and Tilly, respectively."

Tilly hopped up immediately and performed a fully executed curtsy, one befitting a queen. Sadie, on the other hand, grudgingly dipped in a quick and barely acceptable greeting.

Kate bowed her head, hoping the heat in her cheeks was not as flaming red as they felt. Luckily, Nora had drawn Lady Jersey's full attention.

"So, you are the mysterious young lady who has cast a spell over young Weatherford? We'd all written him off as irredeemable. You've created quite a stir, child." She turned to Honore. "Matrons of the *ton* are talking of little else this morning. Indeed, I've had no less than a dozen notes of inquiry. Everyone who's anyone is dying to know, '*Who is this niece of Lady Alameda's who has stolen the heart of the season's most-elusive bachelor?*' A bachelor so clever at avoiding matchmaking mamas, he'd been all but scratched from the eligible lists. '*Should I send the young lady invitations?*' debutantes' mothers asked. '*Oh, tell us, what shall we do?*'

"What shall we do, indeed?" Lady Jersey produced a lorgnette from her seemingly bottomless sleeve. She reached for Nora's hand, urged the girl to her feet, and promptly began to inspect the young lady in question.

Aunt Honore laughed at her friend's speech. "How do you put up with all those mewling cats?"

"What sort of cats are those?" Tilly asked.

"Quiet," Kate warned, for the nineteen-trillionth time.

Lady Jersey didn't seem to mind Tilly's confusion. She turned to the child and, without employing quite as many elongated vowels as usual, offered an explanation of sorts. "If you must know, child, jealousy makes sly cats of some people. They circle round and round their rival's ankles, rubbing and purring as if they're friendly, when what they would rather do is scratch their competition's eyes out."

"Except they haven't the backbone," added Aunt Honore.

Tilly's little face puckered up as she digested this cryptic proverb.

"Smile." Lady Jersey resumed her inspection of Nora. "Good, you have all your teeth. Hhmm." She turned the girl around and continued examining her as if she were a prize pony at an auction. Satisfied, at last, Lady Jersey sat down again and addressed Aunt Honore. "Well, Honore, I believe you may have outdone yourself this time. She'll do."

Lady Alameda shrugged and inspected her fingernails. "Unintentional, I assure you. There's the chit I'm saddled with bringing out." She aimed her pointer finger at Kate.

Saddled?

Her stomach squeezed into an even tighter knot.

An albatross. That's what Kate felt like. She'd read about how sailors disliked the big, unlucky birds. Except, never having actually seen an albatross, Kate decided she felt more like a swayback nag at a pony show.

"Ahh, well, no matter. Everyone loves a challenge." Lady Jersey clapped her hands. "Now, pour us some tea, my lady. All this work in one morning has left me famished. And a scone or two would not go amiss either."

"Or perhaps a cake!" Tilly giggled with delight. "Wait till you try one of the little confections Lord Weatherpuss brought. They're heavenly!"

Honore poured tea for Lady Jersey and frowned at Tilly. "Don't you have some sewing to do? Or a closet to sit in somewhere?"

Tilly shrugged, ignoring her aunt's ire. She opened the box of cakes with a flourish and offered one to their guest. "That one has cream in the middle."

Lady Jersey bit into the confection and narrowed her gaze at Kate. After she finished chewing, she pointed to an empty chair. "Do stop fidgeting, Miss Linnet. Come here and sit down before you do yourself an injury. For heaven's sake, I've already seen the color of your stockings. There's nothing you can do about it now."

Kate dragged herself into the chair. "I don't normally look so . . . so . . ."

"Bedraggled?" offered Lady Jersey.

Kate groaned. "I suppose."

Lady Jersey magically produced a fan out of her other sleeve. "As to that, if I am to grant this one vouchers to Almack's . . ." She waved her closed fan over Nora's head as if it were a wand bestowing sparkling wishes. "I will also need to grant vouchers for you, else it would mean your social ruin. An excluded older sister—it just isn't done. Tongues would wag. What's wrong with the older sister, they would wonder. However, I do not hand out vouchers willy-nilly. I have a reputation to maintain. Do you grasp my meaning, young lady?"

Kate wasn't quite sure she did. She nodded, but the quizzical look on her face must've given her away.

Lady Jersey pursed her lips sternly before lowering her voice to a frightening rumble. "*Improve. Your. Game.*" With each word, she struck the air with her fan.

Game? Kate never played games, but she nodded anyway.

Lady Jersey narrowed her eyes. "And there shall be no more of this bedraggled-ness."

Kate feared, any minute, Tilly would correct the grand lady's grammar. She shot a warning glance to her little sister. She needn't have bothered. Tilly gazed adoringly at Lady Jersey while reverently mouthing the word, "Bedraggled-ness."

Kate bowed her head. "Yes, my lady. I understand."

"I'm not sure you do. You sigh and sigh as if you are a crone of fifty-five rather than a young lady of middle age." Lady Jersey dabbed a bit of frosting from the corner of her mouth.

"Two and twenty, my lady. I am only two and twenty."

"As I said, middle age." She sniffed and surveyed the sweet in her fingers. "Oh my! These are tasty little concoctions." She swallowed the last of the tiny cream cake. "I believe I shall have another."

Tilly obligingly held out the box of cakes. "Try a chocolate one, my lady. Even jealous cats would like that one."

"I believe they would. Too bad *you're* not of age." Lady Jersey laughed and rapped her fan against Tilly's arm. "Saucy minx. Daresay when you *are*, you'll be a handful."

"Already is," Kate muttered.

"And stop muttering as if you're the child's mother. Young ladies do not mutter." Lady Jersey ceased scolding and took a generous bite of chocolate cake.

Not the child's mother?

The words stung.

Stung hard.

A hot, burning barb that shot straight into Kate's soul. She sucked in a trembling breath and clasped her hands in her lap.

Lady Jersey was right.

Except, on second thought, she wasn't. Kate looked up

indignantly. Who had held baby Tilly through the night? Apart from a small respite here and there from the cook and the housemaid, it had been Kate who rocked the child. Kate who fed her warmed goat milk, kept her swaddled, changed, and warm. Kate who taught the baby her first words and how to walk.

For all intents and purposes, she *was* Tilly's mother.

Vouchers or no vouchers, reigning queen of high society or not, Kate was just about to read Lady Jersey a piece of her mind when the butler entered the room. "M'lady, another young gentleman has called. A Lord Colter. Rather insistent fellow. Claims he is expected, and that Miss Linnet requested he take her driving in the park this afternoon."

Greyson?

He came! He called on her, even though she'd made no request to take her to the park or anywhere else.

"Oh, did she now? And who is this Lord Colter?" Lady Jersey seemed quite comfortable interfering in family affairs.

Lady Alameda bent close beside Lady Jersey's ear. She whispered some salacious something that made her guest's eyes widen as if she'd just awakened from a startling dream. "Oh my! Well, in that case, show the gentleman in. I should like to have a look at him." Lady Jersey's lorgnette reappeared from her magical sleeve, but then she glanced at Kate and horror overtook her features. The lorgnette dropped in her lap. "You cannot go out in public like that. I won't have it."

Kate dared to protest. "It is only the park, my lady. Surely—"

"*Only* the park!" Her fan reemerged, and Lady Jersey fanned herself violently. "Miss Linnet, one does not go to the park to see the grass and trees, one goes to *be seen*. Honore, do something!"

Unused to seeing their aunt ordered about by anyone, the girls sat open-mouthed as Honore rang the bell. Cairn turned on his heel and rushed back into the room with surprising speed for so elderly a fellow. "Yes, m'lady."

"Send Lorraine to Miss Linnet's room. Tell her she must do her best to make a silk purse out of this sow's ear." She waved him off to do his duty. "And you, Kate, come. You must slip out the side door and take the back stairs up to your room. There will undoubtedly be a servant who can show you the way."

Kate stood but had no idea what side door her aunt meant.

Honore sighed. "Must I do everything?" She strode across the room and opened a camouflaged servants' door. "Don't stand there gawking like a country bumpkin. Go! And hurry up about it."

Kate scurried into the stairwell, and just as the door closed, she heard her Aunt exclaim, "Lord Colter! What a surprise to see you back so soon for more punishment. Miss Linnet will be down in a few minutes. And may I present to you—"

Kate only caught the beginnings of the introductions before the door clicked shut. She wound up the dimly lit backstairs, completely lost her bearings, and at one point felt doomed to wander endlessly until happening upon a 'tween-stairs maid. The girl graciously led the way to Kate's bedchamber.

Kate stepped into her bedroom and found it brimming with maids. In the middle of this bustling crew stood a small, gnome-like woman whose oversized bun bobbled atop her head like a peculiar hat. "Ah! There you are." She bustled straight for Kate and dipped a quick curtsy. "I'm Lorraine, your aunt's lady's maid."

So this was Aunt Honore's personal dresser, and apparently master sergeant of the troop of maids swirling about the room, sorting through Kate's trunks, hanging garments, and folding stockings. The little woman tugged Kate's elbow. "Let's have a look at you. Good bones. High cheeks. Coloring is pleasant enough. If only ye weren't so washed out. We must do something about that. Oh, but my dear, your hair. Tch, tch." She strained up on her toes. "Sit here, miss, if you please."

Lorraine indicated a small dressing stool, and before Kate had even sat down all the way, the woman pulled out three hairpins and Kate's hair tumbled to her shoulders. "Saints preserve us," Lorraine mourned, removing more pins and hefting Kate's tangled locks. "This is quite a shambles."

She snapped her fingers and two girls promptly appeared at her side. "Sally, we'll need both brushes and water—*tout de suite.* Dora, bring milady's pomade, three pearl combs, and . . ." She frowned, examining Kate's cheeks, hands, and fingers. "The rouge pot, cucumber creams, apricot oil, the pumice files, buffing boards, and a pair of lace gloves, no open fingertips."

Lorraine smiled sympathetically at Kate. "Do you do all your own gardening, my dear? And . . ." She ran her fingers over Kate's palm. "And cleaning?"

"Yes. I mean, no. That is to say, we have a cook and a housemaid."

"*One* maid. I *see.*" Lorraine patted Kate's shoulder sympathetically. "Never you mind, we shall have you presentable in no time."

Presentable?

Cruel truth kicked Kate in the belly. Her shoulders sagged. She would not be the belle of London after all. She was a farm girl with unrealistic aspirations. More than that, she was a mother to her little sister. A bedraggled nobody. What place could she hope to attain in London society? None. *Presentable* was the highest praise to which she could rightfully aspire.

Her eyes burned with humiliation.

"What's all this?" Lorraine leaned her face down a few inches from Kate's. "There, there, miss. It's not as bad as all that. We'll have ye fixed up quick as a wink. No need to cry."

"I'm not. I never cry—"

"Course not. You're a brave lass. Glad to hear it. Puffy eyes are a mite tricky to disguise."

Kate hardly noticed her morning gown being removed. It wasn't until Lorraine pinched the sleeve of her undergarments and sniffed that Kate awakened from her stupor.

"These will need to be changed," declared the dictatorial gnome.

Stripped down to nothing, Kate was scrubbed, plucked, and pumiced, garbed in fresh underclothes, and laced into a corset that scarcely allowed her to breathe. They brushed her hair until not a tangle remained, then twisted, coiled, pinned, and applied pomades and sticky starches. With a pair of hot iron rods, they created tiny ringlets around her face. Dresses of various colors were held next to her cheek until Field Marshall Lorraine finally approved a sky-blue satin gown. It slid over Kate's skin like a cool, luxurious wind. "Does this belong to my aunt?"

"Nay, this was originally made for your cousin, Miss Fiona Hawthorne. Begging your pardon, I should've referred to her as Lady Wesmont, as that is who she is now."

"You knew my cousin?"

"I should say so. The lady saved my life. I would've drowned if it weren't for her. A fine, brave lass like yourself." She smiled as if recalling a fond memory. "You and she are similar in shape and size. The dress suits you."

Kate rubbed the fabric between her fingers. "It's heavenly."

Lorraine crooked her finger at one of the maids. "Bring the lace shawl and the rouge pot." She arranged the lace over Kate's shoulders. "Yes, that will do. And now let us remedy your wan coloring. Sit." She dabbed two spots of pink on Kate's cheekbones and spread the color until it scarcely showed. "There. You do not look so tired and drawn. Stand."

Lorraine made Kate turn as she surveyed her handiwork. At last, she sniffed and made her final pronouncement. "There. That will do. You may go down to the drawing room, miss. You are now ready for the park."

The park.

Kate had never been this *ready* for the assembly ballroom back in Clapsforth-on-Wye.

She descended Aunt Honore's marble staircase, wondering if even her sisters would recognize her. From the foyer, she overheard them chattering. Lady Jersey's voice rang above the others. "My dear boy, you must attend Almack's ballroom this Wednesday. I shall see to it you are admitted. So charming a gentleman will be a welcome addition to our liiiiittle club."

Little club. Ha! Almack's was the pinnacle of London society.

Kate paused outside the drawing room, unsure she—*being merely presentable*—dared to enter. She wasn't ready for this world of false humility and parks that weren't parks but parades for the vain. She had half a mind to turn around, pack her things, buy a ticket on a mail coach, and return home.

Cairn walked up behind her and startled her. "I shall announce you, miss."

"No," she answered a little too vehemently. "Thank you. It's not necessary."

But the old fellow flung the doors open and bowed her in. "Miss Linnet."

Lady Jersey raised her lorgnette and one eyebrow. Sadie took one look and nearly choked on a bite of cake. Nora drew back as if surprised. Aunt Honore, too, almost smiled. Well, sort of— her lips wriggled with wicked delight. "Hhmm," she said, as if calculating her next move in a rather sneaky game of chess.

Lord Colter stood. He blinked, then remembered his manners and bowed his head but quickly looked up. "Kate, er, Miss Linnet, you look . . ."

Tired?

Bedraggled?

"Presentable?" Kate supplied hopefully.

Tilly ran to her and touched the blue satin. "Ooohh."

"She'll do." Lady Jersey set down her lorgnette. "Well, young man, do you intend to stand there all day gawking or are you going to take Miss Linnet for a drive in the park?"

"I, er . . . yes. The horses are standing. Shall we go?"

Kate noticed how carefully he moved his arm. "Your curricle is here in town already?"

"Yes, the inn sent it around this morning." He held out his arm for her to take.

"And are you quite certain you're well enough to drive it? I mean, with your injured shoulder, perhaps you ought not—"

"Drove here, didn't I?" He bristled.

"Yes. I suppose, but—"

"Shall we?" He lengthened his stride so that she had to hurry to keep from being dragged. Just before bolting out of the front door, she overheard Lady Jersey ask, "Does she often needle others in that manner?"

"Oh, noooo," Honore answered. "She's usually much worse."

_Chapter 13
My Fair Farm Girl

GREYSON TOOK UP the reins, and the curricle jogged pleasantly over the cobblestones of her aunt's quiet street. A block later, his ire seemed to abate and he turned to Kate wearing a boyish smile. "I meant to say this earlier, Kate: You look lovely."

He's only saying it to be kind.

Kate pursed her lips and sniffed irritably. "I have it on good authority that I am merely presentable."

"Folderol! Whose authority?" He slapped the horses into a trot.

"Lady Alameda's maid said as much, and I believe her. Mind you, she meant that I am only presentable enough for the park. What's more, she is taking into account the fact that I am a country bumpkin who must toil through life with only one housemaid and a cook."

Having driven onto a much busier street, he turned his attention back to the horses. "She didn't say all that, surely? A maid would never be so bold."

"She did," Kate insisted. "*Nearly*. Well, she inferred as much. And Lorraine is not just any maid. She is Aunt Honore's lady's maid. Apparently, her position makes her equal in rank to General Wellington. The woman took one look at my hands and instantly pitied me on account of my being such a provincial farm girl and all." Kate tried not to frown. It would not do her *merely presentable* appearance any good to compound it with a grumpy expression.

A disapproving grunt rumbled from Greyson's chest. "She's wrong," he huffed. "I like your hands. They show you're a girl who knows how to work when the need arises, yet they're still shapely and graceful."

Her heart sat up a tiny bit higher in her chest at those words. She studied him for a moment, noting the way his cheek muscles flexed so seriously. Then she glanced down at her pitiable hands disguised in the frilly lace gloves. Hands that did, *indeed*, know how to work when the need arose—as it often did.

He interrupted her thoughts with a cluck of his tongue to the horses. "Nothing provincial about you, Kate." He patted her hand before giving the reins a slap and swerving sharply around a dray stopped in traffic.

Kate grabbed the seat, preparing for a collision with an oncoming coach. She sucked in her breath, biting her tongue to keep from crying out for him to drive with more caution. "Goodness!" she yelped, unable to exhale as they passed so close to the coach that their wheels almost touched. "There certainly are a great many more vehicles on the roads here in London."

He slowed his equipage but said nothing.

She pressed her hand over her thumping heart and returned to her former subject. "It wasn't just the maid who commented on my appearance. Lady Jersey ordered me to stop looking so bedraggled."

"Bedraggled?"

"Yes." Kate flicked back one of the annoying ringlets tickling her cheek. "According to her, I behave like an old woman instead of a young girl."

He didn't say anything, so she glanced sideways and saw him frowning. "It's true, then?"

"No!" He stiffened as if caught in a trap. "Not at all. You? An old woman? Not a bit of it. I was simply trying to figure out what she might've meant by a comment like that."

Kate puckered. *She shouldn't have told him what Lady Jersey said.* Except Lord Colter was her best friend, and she'd grown accustomed to telling him whenever something vexed her.

Oh well, too late now. In for a penny, in for a pound.

"I can tell you exactly why she said it." Kate sighed heavily and confessed the worst of it. "Lady Jersey insists I should stop behaving as if I am Tilly's mother."

Greyson looked over at her, his face darkened and his mouth tensed, as if she'd just relayed horrific news. He wheeled the curricle into a quiet lane, away from passersby, and stopped beneath a towering old elm.

"How, Kate?" He leaned in and reached for her hand. "How does Lady Jersey expect you to do that? You are the closest thing to a mother the child has ever known." He clasped her hand tighter. "To do so would not only be wrong—it would be cruel."

She nodded and lowered her eyes, biting her lip against the confusion battling in her chest. "Then . . . what am I to do?" She turned her face up to his, pleading for help. "How am I to behave as if I'm a carefree debutante when I am, in reality, a mother?"

Don't pity me.

Please, whatever you do, don't turn those eyes of concern into useless saucers of pity.

He didn't.

Greyson's eyes changed, but not in the manner she feared they would. His expression melted into an inviting warmth, a warmth that flooded over her, wrapping around her like a cloak on a cold winter's day. And if he'd shouted "*I love you*" so loudly it shook the upper branches of the elm, she wouldn't have believed it nearly as much as she did the expression darkening his eyes while at the same time making them glisten like stars.

He loved her.

Her.

Kate—half mother, half lost girl.

He *understood* and loved her anyway.

If she'd waited, Greyson would have kissed her. She was sure of it. But Kate couldn't, wouldn't, didn't wait. She kissed him. She couldn't help it.

She flung herself forward and pressed her lips against his. Then, in her haste, she peppered him with tiny pecks of gratitude until he wrapped an arm around her and covered her wandering mouth with his. She relaxed into his embrace, reveling in the way he devoured her lips.

For one blissful moment, she was neither a mother nor a lost girl. She was simply a woman.

"Kate," he said breathlessly. "We ought not—"

She silenced him with another kiss. And then another.

Who knows where it would've ended if a gentleman passing by hadn't rapped his cane against the carriage and harrumphed loudly, "Young man!"

"Oh! Right." Greyson pulled back, his cheek reddening as he resituated himself. "My apologies, sir." He flicked the reins, made a clicking noise to his horses, and the curricle jolted into motion, speeding down the lane.

"Well, I am not sorry. Not one bit." Kate crossed her arms with considerable irritation. "The old goat interrupted the most pleasant moments I've had in recent memory. I shan't apologize for that."

"More where that came from," muttered Greyson. In a louder voice, he asked, "You must admit it was improper. If that gentleman had known your father, I daresay, by nightfall, we'd be standing in front of a priest reciting wedding vows. Not that I would mind. I take it this means you'll reconsider our engagement?"

Did it? Is that what that kiss meant?

Those kisses. In her mind, she could hear Tilly correcting her.

What did those kisses mean?

Marriage?

No. No! Not yet. She wasn't ready for that. It's why they'd been engaged for two years without setting a date. It might even explain why she constantly picked at him. She knew what marriage meant. More obligations. Managing an additional household. No doubt, babies would follow. Kate groaned softly, slumping under the thought of more responsibilities heaped on her shoulders. On the other hand, neither did she want to lose Greyson.

She massaged her forehead with lace-covered fingers. "I don't know," she mumbled.

"What?" He gave a terse click to his team, and the bays trotted around an elderly woman plodding along in a dogcart harnessed to an equally ancient mule.

"I need time to think." She didn't intend for her answer to come out sounding like a petulant child's, yet it did.

"I see," he snapped before she could explain. "Blast it all, Kate! Do you mean to tell me, after all that—back there." He jabbed his hand back toward the towering elm they'd left behind. "After kissing me so warmly—you still want time to think?"

She edged away from him. "I—I . . . You don't understand."

"Oh, I understand well enough. I'm a fool. And you're toying with my affections."

"No!" She drew back as if he'd slapped her.

Toying with his affections? Didn't he realize the whirlwind of emotions raging inside her? "How can you say such a thing? I would never—"

"Oh, but you would, Kate. You do! You've been twisting my heart into knots for nigh onto two years. One minute, you look at me as if I'm the only man in the world, as if I'm a ruddy knight of the round table. The next, you act as if spending your life with me would be a loathsome burden."

"Not loathsome, but . . . but . . . a burden nonetheless. Surely you understand? Babies might come along." Her cheeks flamed with embarrassment, but it had to be said. "Along with a hundred other responsibilities. I . . . I'm just not ready." She reached for his arm.

Greyson jerked away as if her fingertips scorched him. "That's what love is, Kate. Accepting the difficulties along with the good. If you loved me, you'd be willing to face those burdens. We'd take them on together. But it's clear you don't love me."

The hurt twisting his features made Kate blink with shame.

"You don't," he echoed softly. "And that explains why you're forever picking at me."

"No," she squeaked defensively. "I pick at everyone."

He shook his head but said nothing.

"It's not as if I singled you out for that honor. I needle everyone. Ask my sisters. Ask anyone. Even Lady Jersey noticed it."

At his mulish silence, Kate caught her bottom lip between her teeth. And to keep from clutching at his arm, clasped her hands in her lap.

His jaw buckled tighter with each passing minute. Suddenly, he wheeled the curricle around, turning sharply right in the middle of the road. An oncoming horse reared, nearly throwing its rider. A phaeton narrowly skirted past them.

"Greyson!" Kate shrieked and fought to calm her wildly beating heart. "Good heavens. Have a care."

"Caring seems to be my downfall," he said, without so much as a glance in her direction. Then he fixed his lips together in a hard, unbending line.

They were no longer going to the park.

_Chapter 14
Jealousy Is in the Eye of the Beholder

KATE TRUDGED UP the steps of her aunt's Grecian-temple townhouse as would a downcast sinner plodding into a cathedral. The door opened, and she was met with a flurry of activity. Housemaids and footmen scurried every which way, and Aunt Honore stood on the landing directing them.

At Kate's entrance, she blinked in surprise. "You're back sooner than I expected." She scrutinized Kate with an altogether too perceptive squint. "Hhmm. Just as well. The dressmaker is here. You'll need to be fitted. Come along with me."

"Dressmaker?" Kate stepped aside, allowing a footman carrying a chair to mount the stairs ahead of her.

"Naturally," Aunt Honore huffed. "Surely you didn't think you could show up at Almack's wearing those homespun frocks you wore back home in Clappity-Clap-Clap . . . Where is it again?"

"Clapsforth-on-Wye."

"Never heard of it."

She most certainly had heard of it.

"You were in Clapsforth not two days ago." Kate let her gaze drift up to the soaring heights of Aunt Honore's domed roof.

"Was I? Huh. So that's what they call that muddy-puddle village." Aunt Honore sniffed as they rounded the second flight of stairs. "Nevertheless, I shan't be seen with country dowds. I have a reputation to defend."

"Don't you mean a reputation to *maintain*?"

"Piffle. I always say exactly what I mean. What's more, you're beginning to sound like that troublesome little sister of yours. I meant *defend*. You shall see why when you meet the competition at Almack's this Wednesday."

"Wednesday—this week? So soon? We'll never be ready. And anyway, I'm not sure I care to attend."

"What?" Aunt Honore stopped on the stairs and clasped Kate's arm. "Is that cowardice I smell? Because I don't allow the stink of spinelessness upon anyone related to me."

"I'm not a coward! I simply don't see the point in attending a ball."

"Oh, you don't, do you?" Honore's nostrils flared. "Well then, allow me to illuminate you."

Kate groaned. "I believe you mean illuminate the point."

Honore leaned close with a warning glare, gave Kate's arm a shake, and jerked free. "Are you really so selfish that you would ruin your sisters' chances at happiness?"

"Selfish? Me?" Kate stepped back and gaped at her aunt,

who, by all standards and rumors, was purported to be the most self-serving, mercenary lady in all of England.

"Yes, *you*. Do you really believe Nora or your other sisters will be accepted anywhere if you are not? Do you think anyone will believe you'd prefer to stay home and read a book rather than attend the most exclusive social club in the world? Fah!" Honore leaned against the railing and crossed her arms. "It will take the cackle hens in the *beau monde* less than three minutes to dream up some sort of scandal. They'll have you down as damaged goods by the end of the first half hour. And judging by how red and swollen your lips are, I might be inclined to agree with them."

Oh no! Were they swollen?

Kate's hands flew to her lips. "But no, I-I'm not . . . We weren't . . . He—"

She clamped her traitorous lips shut to keep from stuttering like a three-year-old. For pity's sake, Tilly could lie with more finesse. Kate marshaled her tongue and faced her aunt. "You mistake the matter."

"Humph. I am rarely mistaken. Rarely. I comprehend a great deal more than you think, my dear. And that brings us to another reason why you must go to the ball, my poor darling Cinderella." Honore's arms relaxed to her sides, and she squinted at Kate with one brow arched expectantly. "*He'll* be there."

"He will?"

Checkmate.

Honore's lips spread in a slow-curling, evil grin. "Oh yes, my dear. *He* will be there, as will about eighty of the most beautiful gels in England, along with their matchmaking mamas. All of whom have heard by now that Lord Colter is an excessively wealthy baron newly come to town in search of a bride to set up in his sprawling estate just outside of—where is it now? Oh, yes, Clapsforth."

"But . . ." Kate's stomach churned uncomfortably, which was remarkable considering how empty it was. Then the blasted thing balled up like a prickly hedgehog. She pressed her hand over the stupid organ in an effort to calm it down. "But . . . I don't understand." She shook her head.

"What are you failing to understand? Greedy mamas? Or the eighty debutantes who will find your curly-haired Lord Colter infinitely more attractive than the bald, old suitors their mothers have currently inked onto their dance cards?" Aunt Honore watched Kate shrewdly.

"No, no." Kate swatted at her aunt's words. "Why would they think he's rich? Lord Colter isn't wealthy, not by London standards. Oh, he has a modest income. Better than Papa's, but not by much. And his estate is pleasant enough, some sheep, corn and wheat fields, but I wouldn't call it sprawling. What gave them the impression he is rich?"

"I've no idea how these rumors start." Aunt Honore shrugged. "What does it matter? Most of them will find his title and a few sheep perfectly acceptable. Daresay he'll be off your hands in no time. Tell you what, I'll lay you odds he won't last two weeks before one of those eager little princesses snaps him up. Prize of the marriage mart, they're calling him."

It was then Kate realized she was beginning to breathe heavily, like a dragon about to spit fire. "You did this!"

"Oh, pooh. I've done nothing."

"You started the rumor."

"Me? I haven't left the house all morning."

"You whispered something to Lady Jersey, didn't you?"

Aunt Honore resumed her pace up the stairs. "I don't see what all the fuss is about. You wanted to be rid of him. Consider yourself ridden."

"*Rid*," Kate growled. "Consider myself rid of him." Although truth be told, she felt as if she'd just been ridden straight off a cliff.

"Exactly." Honore patted her hand against the railing. "There you are. You're welcome. He's gone from your life, straight into the arms of some simpering little twit. You needn't give him another thought. You're free." Honore fluttered her hand through the air like a bird flying away.

Except Kate didn't want to be rid of him. She wasn't a free-fluttering bird. She was a seething dragon. The thought of some girl with lily-white hands—hands that had never known a day's work—touching his face or his mouth or any other part of him made her boil. She felt like blasting a hole in her aunt's pristine white walls. She wanted to scorch her interfering aunt's skirts with flames. Worst of all, she knew for a fact she didn't want to be rid of Greyson.

Not *now*.

Not *ever*.

She had less than two weeks to get him back. "All right. I'll go. But we still have the problem of Wednesday. We'll never be ready in time for Almack's."

"Won't we?" Honore threw open the doors of the upstairs parlor. Kate wondered for a moment if she'd stepped into a sewing shop. A half dozen seamstresses perched on chairs and stools around the room, bent intently over their stitching. Two more women were measuring and pinning fabric on Nora, who stood in the center of all this industry like a goddess on a pedestal.

A lady in an elegant Turkish turban strolled through the seamstresses and stopped in front of Nora. "Try gold filigree muslin. Yes, yes, *oui*. Ziz is lovely next to her skin. Keep the neckline like so—not too low, but just low enough. You see?" She nodded sagely at the woman draping fabric over Nora's shoulder. "Silver embroidery around the hem. *Très bien*."

"*That* is Madame Brigitte." Honore pointed out the turbaned lady. "The most ingenious dressmaker in all of London. Her real name is Ada Bainbridge, but you mustn't call her that. Ladies of the ton think only a French modiste will do. I discovered her stitching her marvelous creations in Tottenham, of all places. Nonetheless, the woman is brilliant, as you will soon see."

Madame Brigitte approached them and bobbed a quick curtsy to Lady Alameda, and Honore introduced Kate. Madame assessed her thoughtfully. "*Enchantée*, Miss Linnet." She turned with a quizzical frown to Aunt Honore. "But I do not comprehend your warning that she would be difficult. Her figure is fine, and ze coloring *charmante*."

Honore's nose tilted higher. "I was not referring to her appearance."

Kate's head began to throb. Today had already turned into the second-worst day of her life, and here she'd only thought it was the third-worst. She needed to take control. Kate shoved her shoulders back and marched into battle. "Aunty, you are frightening Madame Brigitte." She bestowed a smile on the worried dressmaker that, hopefully, looked halfway genuine.

"Ugh. I don't like the sound of that. You must never call me

'Aunty' again. 'My lady' will do."

"As you wish, Aunty." Kate ignored her aunt, huffing like an enraged hen, and continued to greet the dressmaker. "I'm certain the two of us will get along splendidly."

"*Mais oui*. But of course." Ada Bainbridge, er, Madame Brigitte winked. "Come this way, *mademoiselle*. I know just the *fabrique* for you."

Kate didn't have the heart to mention that Ada was using *fabrique* incorrectly, and when the woman swirled a luxurious silk over Kate's shoulder, she no longer cared two figs about Madame Brigitte's French misstep. "It's . . . it is—"

"*Magnifique*, no?"

"Oh, yes." Kate fingered the silk reverently. "*Magnifique*, indeed."

"It is perfect for you. Full of surprises." Madame held up a length of the shot silk. "See how in ziz light it appears shell pink, almost an innocent creamy peach, but then it shifts and—*voilà!* We see ze alluring red blush."

Aunt Honore stood behind Kate and cleared her throat with considerable irritation. "Ada, an extraordinary fabric like this—I should have thought you would reserve for me, your benefactor."

"Ahh, *excusez-moi*, my lady. But *non*. This is a clever silk, yes, suitable for a young lady who is a cut above ze ordinary debutante. But for ze great lady such as yourself, I have reserved something bolder, more daring."

"More daring?" Honore's eyes flashed with greed.

Madame smirked slyly. "But of course." With a flourish, she drew out a bolt of midnight blue silk and unfurled it. When it caught the light, portions of the evening blue shimmered with a deep wine color hidden in the folds.

"Oh my!" Kate's hand flew to her bosom. "I had no idea such fabrics existed."

A seamstress seated nearby lifted her eyes from her work and sighed with admiration.

Nora spoke up from her perch atop a stool. "It's magical."

"Yes, bewitching," Honore whispered, smoothing her palm over the fascinating silk.

"*Exactamente*. Now, *s'il vous plait*, if you will come with me," Madame crooked her finger, "I will show you *ze* patterns I have drawn up for you."

"Remarkable." Wednesday evening, Kate stood in front of a mirror wearing the soft pink shot silk. She had never worn anything so fine and beautiful. It flowed over her torso as if angels had sewn it on her at birth.

Lorraine and her bevy of soldiers had coiffed and curled Kate's hair, artfully winding a string of pearls through her honey-colored locks. They had dressed her neck with a simple gold locket and Lorraine had explained, "We would not want anything to distract from this exquisite gown." At that, Kate realized she was merely the post upon which it was displayed.

Would the guests at Almack's tonight notice the dress or her, Kate wondered. She turned from side to side, watching the colors shift from soft pink to rose in the light. Madame Brigitte was truly a genius. It was daring, to say the least, but it flattered her figure and brought out the pink in her cheeks. The ballgown made her feel as if she were in possession of a dangerous secret.

"You look very pretty." Tilly lay sprawled haphazardly across the bed, her head hanging off so that she viewed Kate upside down.

"Under the covers, you. It is time for all imps to be asleep." She kissed her beloved little imp on the forehead and tucked the covers around her.

Tilly reached out and grabbed Kate's hand. "Promise you won't marry anyone. Lord Colter would've been all right because he lives close by. But seeing as that is all done and over, no one else, Katie. Promise."

"It's Nora who has the gentlemen swooning over her, not me. You needn't worry, mouse. Now go to sleep." Kate chucked Tilly's chin.

"Time to go." Nora stood in the doorway, looking for all the world like a fairytale princess. "We mustn't be late. Almack's closes its doors at precisely eleven o'clock. Aunt Honore said Lady Jersey turned away General Wellington himself, and he was only seven minutes late."

"Well, I suppose rules are rules. Let us be off." Kate turned out the lantern and swallowed a lump of apprehension. If she held Nora's hand a little tighter than usual as they hurried down the stairs, it didn't mean she had a case of the nerves. She was simply protecting her sister.

_Chapter 15
Dangerous Wallflowers

A T ALMACK'S, KATE and Nora presented their vouchers to the doorman, although he might've been a sentry. Kate wasn't sure of the stern fellow's position, but it was clear no one was getting past him without the proper papers. Once inside those hallowed doors, Kate took inventory of their crowded surroundings. There were so many people crammed into the assembly hall that it scarcely left enough room to dance, certainly not enough to perform the steps properly.

And it was hot—dreadfully hot and stuffy. Lady Jersey and the other patronesses sat enthroned on a raised dais at the far end of the assembly room. At the other end, Kate spied a balcony overlooking the dance floor and the musicians' platform. She made a mental note to locate the stairs and escape to that lofty hiding place. The main floor seemed aflutter with ostrich feathers and glimmering silk. Indeed, nearly every female had two or three frothy plumes sprouting from her head—everyone except Kate. The simple string of pearls adorning her hair seemed rather understated in the present company.

Nora rocked up on her toes, surveying the gathering, and clasped her hands together. "Oh, Katie! Isn't it glorious?"

Kate was about to answer that it looked as if they'd been invaded by a flock of large birds, but Aunt Honore beat her to it. "Glorious? Humph. Only if you enjoy a gaggle of flamingos flapping about your ballroom."

"Not a gaggle, Aunt." Kate corrected without thinking. "It is geese who congregate in gaggles. One refers to a flock of flamingos as . . . a . . ." Her words drifted into oblivion as a cluster of ostrich feathers parted momentarily revealing Lord Colter, laughing and smiling, basking in the center of attention. A dozen adoring young females surrounded him, and Kate felt as if a gaggle of something had just flown down her throat.

Aunt Honore nudged Kate. "Do close your mouth, dear. Bound to attract flies."

Nora still clutched Kate's arm. "Oh look, Kate, there's Lord Colter. My, but he looks dashing tonight. Don't you think so?"

"Yes." Aunt Honore responded for Kate, who still stood gaping. "Astonishing what brushing one's hair will accomplish."

"Perhaps we ought to greet him?" Nora suggested. "He seems to know a prodigious number of people. Do you think he might introduce us?"

Kate could only back away, shaking her head.

"Ah, there you are, Miss Linnet." Lord Weatherpain strode up and bowed to Nora, Kate, and Lady Alameda. He quickly introduced his two companions and turned back to Nora. "I've been beside myself awaiting your arrival. Can't abide these sorts of events. Only came in the hope of seeing you tonight. And may I say, you look lovely—nay, radiant. Drat it all, words fail me in your presence. If only my friend, Lord Byron, were here. He might be able to put words to your beauty."

The younger of his companions shook his head. "No. Daresay even Byron would have difficulty finding the right words." The fellow seemed as enamored with Nora's charms as did Lord Weatherpest.

"Oh, for pity's sake!" Lady Alameda snorted rather obnoxiously. "Anyone would think Aphrodite had returned to earth."

"Exactly!" Lord Weatherwit's finger shot into the air. "That's it. You are Aphrodite returned to us." Three more gentlemen gathered around Nora and Nitwit Neddy. There was a small argument about which of the gentleman deserved the honor of fetching a cup of ratafia punch for Nora.

Honore sighed. "There was a day when it was I who . . . Never mind." She collapsed her fan and rapped it against her thigh. "Come along, Kate. I've had all I can tolerate of this nonsense. Would you care to accompany me up to that balcony you keep eyeing?"

Kate did not have a chance to answer.

"I would be pleased to accompany you, as well." His voice was low and sultry, and to be honest, Kate couldn't recall the name by which the gentleman had been introduced. Mr. Smythe, was it? To be fair, Neddy had rattled off the name as if it were of no consequence. The gentleman was broad-shouldered, dark-haired, and not bad looking, but brooding in appearance. There was a measure of cynicism in his demeanor. He'd remained standing a pace behind Lord Weatherpit, quietly observing, and Kate hadn't paid him much attention.

"For the record," the fellow said, as they made their way across the crowded room and turned into a passage headed for the stairs, "I know Lord Byron quite well, and he would never have gushed over that young lady. Not his sort of chit, you see."

Chit. Kate winced, and her fingers curled with irritation. "That young lady happens to be my sister, sir. And she is a very good sort, I assure you."

"No doubt," he countered. "She's fair enough, to be sure. But I know from experience Byron has no interest in angelic maids. He prefers a woman with pluck. A woman more like yourself." Kate glanced over her shoulder and noticed the corner of his mouth turning up slyly. "And your fair aunt."

Lady Alameda laughed. "Silver-tongued devil. Mind yourself, Smythe, or I shall have to cuff you with my fan."

"Strike away, my lady. T'would prefer a beating to watching Neddy fall on his knees before yon maiden."

Honore opened her mouth to retort, but they were met on the stair by Lord Monmouth, whom Aunt Honore introduced to Kate as one of her oldest and dearest friends. Kate wondered exactly *how dear* when the nobleman greeted her aunt with an embarrassingly amorous kiss. "Ah, my dear, Lady Alameda. You are just the person I was hoping to see," he rumbled loudly. "You must come outside with me. The air in here is wretchedly close. The smoke from those abominable new gas lamps makes my eyes water. I would be delighted to have your company for a few moments of fresh air on the front steps."

"A few moments? You know perfectly well that if we leave, Lady Jersey won't let us back inside. The doors will be locked."

He clicked his tongue and scratched his side whiskers. "Wretched rules. The patronesses run this place like a veritable fortress. Whitehall should be so well-guarded. I have it! We can leave and wait for your charges in your carriage. You wouldn't mind that, would you, Miss Linnet?"

Yes. Kate minded very much, thank you. She looked aghast at her aunt. "What of Nora? You can't leave her—"

Honore cast her gaze at the ceiling with some irritation. "Nora is far more capable than you credit her. Only look." She gestured flippantly at the crowded room through the doorway. "She is surrounded by so great an army of suitors, one cannot even see her."

"All the more reason for you to watch over her." Kate stared indignantly at Lady Alameda, who was batting her eyelashes shamelessly at Lord Monmouth.

Truthfully, it wasn't only Nora's welfare gnawing at Kate. She caught the corner of her lip, hoping Aunt Honore would not abandon her in this strange place and leave her to fend for herself. Especially not while the man who had Kate's heart tripping in four different directions stood in the next room charming a harem of eligible females.

"I shall be pleased to look after you, Miss Linnet." Kate had nearly forgotten about the tall, dark stranger lurking over her shoulder. "You may depend upon me, my dear."

"There! You see." Honore smiled triumphantly. "Nora has her army of suitors, and you have our good friend, Mr. Smythe."

Mr. Smythe, whom earlier you threatened to swat with your

fan.

"Ta, ta." Honore waggled her fingers in farewell. "We shall await you in the carriage."

"But . . . but that could be hours from now," Kate protested.

Honore laughed. "Not to worry. Lord Monmouth and I shall find a way to pass the time."

"Aunt—" Her plea fell on deaf ears. Kate's outstretched hand dropped to her side. Aunt Honore, true to form, was following her own whims without a thought of others. Kate knew this would happen. Her sisters predicted it. So did Papa. She had no one to blame for this London fiasco except herself. She would simply have to manage this evening on her own.

Honore wandered away laughing and chatting giddily. Mr. Smythe guided Kate up to the balcony overlooking the dance floor. Music from the orchestra swirled up to them in great, booming wafts. Smoke from the oil lamps coiled and eddied through the air in thick tendrils, creating a foggy, mystical sort of Netherland. Kate leaned over the railing, and from that vantage point, she saw Greyson dancing, palm to palm, with a dark-haired beauty. Rich—the girl had to be rich. Three silver ostrich feathers bobbed from her Grecian coiffure and a glittering diamond necklace adorned her throat. An heiress, no doubt, and Greyson seemed so enthralled with her he scarcely glanced up in Kate's direction.

Katie sighed.

She was too late.

Mr. Smythe snaked his arm around Kate's waist. "What seems to be troubling you, my dear?"

Kate stiffened. "At the moment, it is your familiarity, sir. I must ask you to kindly remove your hand." She plucked up his hand as if it were an errant pup and held it away from her waist.

He pulled free, grinning, as if her request gratified him. "Come now, my girl. You are Lady Alameda's niece, are you not? Everyone knows her reputation. You cannot be ignorant of the ways of the world."

"I am neither ignorant nor corrupt, sir. Now, kindly step back."

The wretch smirked and edged closer.

"Step back," she growled, saying it loudly enough that she hoped some other patron might come to her aid.

"Ahh, the kitten has teeth." He laughed and strode shamelessly close. "All the better to play with."

Kitten?

She'd show him how very un-kitten-like she could be. Kate's fists knotted into two tight mallets. She shoved him back. Hard. "I'm not playing!"

She'd wrestled into submission stubborn sheep who didn't want to be sheared, ornery goats who didn't like being milked, and three disobedient sisters who never ever wanted to do as they were told. Kate expected Mr. Smythe would be as wayward as any other goat. She counted on him pressing his luck.

He did precisely as she anticipated. Mr. Smythe lunged for her.

Kate ducked and shoved upward, using his momentum to heave him over the railing. What she didn't count on was him clinging so tightly to her and dragging her halfway over with him.

Chapter 16
Hanging by A Thread

"HELP!" Mr. Smythe screeched like a terrified little girl. "Help!"

He had a bruising grip on one of Kate's arms and a great deal of her frock in his other fist. Indeed, she felt the seams beginning to rip. She gritted her teeth. The blighter would've pulled her over with him had she not jammed her feet through the railings in the nick of time. But her slippers were sliding upward at an alarming pace. To keep him from tearing the top of her gown off entirely, she reached out her hand, hoping he would swap cloth for her fingers. Her hips were sliding dangerously forward.

"My hand, Mr. Smythe. Grab my hand."

He stopped gaping at the floor below and looked up. Panic twisted his features into an ugly grimace.

The music screeched to a halt. Gasps and screams of alarm

pelted the smoky air. Guests scattered from the area below them.

Judging by their horrified expressions, Kate was willing to bet that a couple dangling from the balcony was not a common, everyday occurrence at Almack's. Her gown ripping was bound to catapult the whole debacle into the realm of legendary. She would never be allowed in polite society again.

"Mr. Smythe!" She scolded him as fiercely as she would a naughty child. "Unless you would rather fall to your death, you will take hold of my hand this instant." He wouldn't die. She was only saying that to scare him into doing the reasonable thing. Oh, he might break a leg or two, but falling from that distance wasn't going to kill him.

Common sense flickered briefly in Mr. Smythe's eyes. Surprisingly, he obeyed her and let go of her sleeve—except panic then returned full force. He flailed, swatting wildly at the air before snagging her hand in a crushing, clawing grip.

Kate winced.

She had half a mind to shake him loose rather than let the rascal continue to bruise her. Except she couldn't do that. With a sigh, she tried to heave him up. Trouble was, he was too heavy, and her feet were losing purchase tucked around the railing.

Four gentlemen below were forming a net of sorts. Lord Weatherford had pulled off his coat and was instructing some of his friends to hold the corners. "Jump, Smythe," he shouted up to his friend. "Jump. We'll catch you."

Mr. Smythe's face turned into a mask of terror. "No!" He shouted and turned his anguish up to Kate. "Don't let go. Please. Don't let go."

"It's not that far, sir. Your friends will save you. I haven't the strength to pull you up."

"I do." Lord Colter strode across the balcony, grasped Kate's waist, and pulled her back down to where her feet rested on the floor. Then he leaned next to Kate, reached over the rail with his good arm, and grasped Mr. Smythe. Greyson looked at her—her oldest friend in the world—his eyes alight, half laughing, half shaking his head. "Shall we? *Together*?" he asked.

She smiled. Somehow in the midst of this ludicrous disaster, she felt happier than she had in years. She nodded. "Together."

He nodded. "Ready? Heave-ho!"

And so they did. They yanked the lucky buzzard up and over the rail. Mr. Smythe collapsed in a heap at their feet.

"Smythe?" Greyson frowned at the culprit.

The culprit in question sat up and tapped his forehead as if tipping an imaginary hat. "Pleased to see you, Colter."

"If I'd known it was you—" Greyson crossed his arms. "We should've let you fall on your thick skull."

We.

Hope took flight in her heart, flapping its fragile little wings. Kate did her best to hide her smile.

"Grateful you didn't." Mr. Smythe rubbed his arm sheepishly. "Miss Linnet, a thousand pardons. I entirely misjudged your character." He clambered to his feet and bowed before her. "Can you ever forgive me?"

"I suppose . . ." His contrition embarrassed her until, glancing down, she saw the red marks on her arm. They would turn to purple bruises by morning. "I forgive you, sir. Unfortunately, the incident has done irreparable damage to both our reputations. Especially mine. I suspect I shall be cast in a most unfavorable light."

"Not if I can help it." Mr. Smythe straightened his waistcoat and marched to the railing.

"Here now, Smythe, what are you doing?" Greyson cautioned.

But Mr. Smythe ignored him and raised both arms in triumph. "Huzzah! Ladies and gentlemen, I am alive!"

A cheer went up from the spectators below.

"And I owe it all to this brave young lady." Smythe held out his hands to her. "See how she stands back and blushes. So humble." He tugged Kate forward into the light. "You all saw it. Stumbling oaf that I am, this young lady saved me!" Like a seasoned orator, he raised his voice louder and louder. "Miss Linnet is as brave and kind as she is beautiful. A true hero!"

In front of the entire audience, he bowed lavishly to her. Kate glanced nervously at the guests staring up at them and then at her companions on the balcony. Greyson was brooding, and Mr. Smythe cast her a wry grin before whirling back to the crowd. "All is well! Let the dancing resume!"

"But it's not well," Kate muttered. "Not well at all."

Mr. Smythe smirked at her. "Come now, I believe you will not suffer too much, Miss Linnet. Everyone believes you to be my rescuing angel."

She stamped her foot. "Except none of it was true. Lord Colter saved you, not I. If he had not come to your aid—"

"I came to *your* aid, Kate. Not his," Greyson grumbled.

Mr. Smythe leaned toward her, tapping a finger to his nose as if they were playing charades. "Ah, but consider this, my dear girl. Colter would've arrived too late if you had not first grabbed my hand."

Kate rejected his game with a shake of her head. "No, I only did that because you were tearing my gown—"

"Tearing your gown? What?" Lord Colter clamped his fist around Smythe's arm. "You scoundrel."

"It's not what you think, my good man." Smythe leaned back, warding him off. "And I'm quite certain the young lady would prefer it if you lowered your voice."

Greyson fell silent, but he bore down on Smythe with an expression so savage it made Kate fear he might rip Smythe's throat out.

Despite the threat, Mr. Smythe chattered on pleasantly. "Oh, I admit, there may have been a momentary lapse in judgment on my part, but I assure you, the maiden's honor is completely unscathed. Not so much as even a chaste peck on the cheek passed between us."

Greyson ceased growling, and Mr. Smythe began calmly prying Lord Colter's fingers, one by one, from his arm. "In point of fact, and I am somewhat loath to admit this, I did not stumble. My good man, have you ever known me to be the stumbling sort?" He babbled on as if he and Greyson were old friends.

Unmoved, Greyson crossed his arms and towered over Smythe.

Smythe smiled genially. "No, I didn't stumble. It was the young lady who tossed me over the rail. Don't know how she managed it, but there it is. I have already been punished for my misdeeds."

Lord Colter uncrossed his arms and turned to Kate. "You did this?"

She peered down at the toes of her shoes. "Might've done."

"You see? And now, my friends, I must limp home with my tail tucked, as it were." He bowed gallantly to her. "Miss Linnet, if you don't mind, I shall leave you in the care of this gentleman. Although, if this evening is any indication, you seem amply equipped to watch out for yourself."

True enough. The compliment pleased her, and she decided Mr. Smythe was not an altogether bad sort, after all. "Do stay out of trouble, sir. I should not like to think of you taking another nasty fall."

He had the good grace to laugh.

Greyson's jaw was doing that wicked little dance it always does when he's cogitating—tightening the muscles and loosening them over and over. The moment Mr. Smythe left them, he began lecturing her. "What possessed you, Kate, to come up here with a rake like him?"

"I didn't know he was a rake."

"I don't believe you. You're a better judge of character than that."

She shrugged and decided it was best to tell him the truth, and the crux of it spilled out all at once. "I couldn't bear standing down there, watching you flirting and cavorting with all those beautiful girls."

"I wasn't flirting or cavorting."

"You were."

He didn't deny it again, so she glanced sideways up at him and found him openly studying her. "Even if I were," he said with a frown, "what do you care?"

Scalding heat rushed into her cheeks, giving her away.

The truth. Tell him the truth, her heart screamed.

All right.

Very well.

She would tell him how she felt—that she mourned the thought of not having him in her life. How her heart felt empty and cold without him. Yes, and she ought to confess that, rather than lose him, she might be willing to endure the inevitable burdens of a life together, no matter how torturous.

Might be willing?

Tortuous?

Merciful heavens! She couldn't say all that. It would hurt him again.

Oh, fiddlesticks . . . She didn't know what to say. How could she tell him the truth if she wasn't sure of it herself? Kate felt an insane urge to thump her forehead against the nearby wall.

Instead, she bowed her head and tried in vain to calm her racing thoughts. Her lungs filled with air, and she groped awkwardly for the right words. She searched his face, hoping he would understand without her having to confess the truth. And yet, his stone-like gaze remained fastened on her. He would make her say it. And then what? Would he sneer at her? Mock her fickle-mindedness? Would he let her suffer as she had him?

Kate's mouth opened, but nothing came out. Nothing except fear and confusion—all of it escaping in a whimpered gust. An unintelligible mew.

"That's what I thought." Greyson's shoulders stiffened, and he turned on his heel.

He was leaving her. Walking away. She would be left standing alone in this haze-filled balcony.

No!

"I care." The words barely squeaked out.

She was not brave. Nothing like a hero. She was a mouse. A *stupid, scaredy-cat mouse. No, wait. That isn't right. A mouse can't be a cat—*

He's leaving!

Kate moaned. His every step hurt—physically hurt.

Greyson paused by the doorway, turning only halfway, as if making sure he could hear her in case she said more.

But she stood there, frozen in place, gasping like a frightened rabbit. Her heart hammered so hard it felt as if her chest would burst apart. A hundred things to say flew through her mind.

Don't go.

Stay.

I do care.

I have always cared.

Any of those things might have kept him there. They would all have been true. Any one of them might have made him turn back.

Pick one, her braver self screamed.

Pick one!

Clatters and voices rang from the stairwell. Lady Alameda burst into view, scurrying up the stairs in a mad rush, and beside her came Nora.

"Out of the way, young man." Honore shoved onto the balcony and glanced up at Lord Colter. "Oh, it's you. Humph. I wondered where you'd been all night. You can go. I'm here now." She dismissed him with a flick of her hand. "Oh, my dear, sweet, brave girl! You poor, noble child, how perfectly awful that you had to save that wretched Mr. Smythe."

While she rattled on, Greyson glanced back at Kate. He did not look angry, as she'd feared. He looked disappointed—she had failed him.

Again.

Ignoring her aunt and Nora, who had surrounded her so tightly she couldn't reach out her hand to him, Kate opened her mouth in a silent plea. More people were thumping up the stairs, pouring into the crowded balcony. Lord Monmouth and Lord Weatherford led the pack, barking out shouts of concern, echoing Mr. Smythe's overblown platitudes about Kate's heroic courage. *Her courage,* in truth, was nonexistent.

Lord Colter stood above the crowd, his face an inscrutable mask. With a final frown of farewell, he turned and shoved his way into the stairwell.

Aunt Honore choose that soul-grinding moment to clasp Kate's shoulders, fixing her in place, and loudly declared, "My darling girl! What a fright you gave us. Monmouth and I had only just reached the doors to leave when we heard that awful commotion—for a moment, I thought it was a strangled cat. We were frozen in horror, watching poor Mr. Smythe dangle like a broken earring from the balcony. I daresay you both could've been killed. How fortuitous that you saved him." This last, she nearly shouted, and Kate suspected it was not said for her benefit at all.

Nora stroked Kate's arm soothingly and quietly whispered, "Are you all right, Katie? Truly?"

No. Kate was not *all right.* She was woefully and completely wrong. But the time for truth-telling had slipped through her fingers. "A bit bruised," she managed to say with a forced smile. "That's all."

_Chapter 17
Every Man Must Have His Dog

"**N**O! YOU MAY NOT go home." Aunt Honore seized Kate's wrist in a painful twist and, through gritted teeth, spoke into Kate's ear. "You will stay and dance and take full advantage of the admiration you've garnered. It is not every day an opportunity such as this falls into your lap."

"Or from the balcony," Kate murmured. "Yes, all right. If you wish it, I will stay."

Honore let go of her wrist and sneered. "Oh no, my dear. You mistake me. I do not wish it. I *insist*." The devilish way her aunt hissed the last word was almost frightening. But then, Kate's cowardice was showing off all of its fine white feathers tonight.

She agreed to a country set with the first gentleman who asked. She followed him down to the ballroom floor. He wore a dark green coat, and that was all she noticed or cared to notice. She drifted through the steps of the country reel, all the while searching for the one face above all the others that mattered most.

On the second turn, she finally spotted Lord Colter standing across the room back against the wall. He was glowering at her as if she were the most annoying creature on earth. Kate's partner tapped her on the shoulder to remind her to cross to the corner couple. When she glanced back to where Greyson had been standing, he was gone.

She managed to step through the next two sets as if sleepwalking. Her conversation was sparse. Her partners had to be content with a meek smile from her now and then—that is, when she remembered to do it. Most of the time, she was peering out at the crowd, hunting for the one face that could make everything all right again.

He seemed to have vanished.

And now, he was not merely gone from her life, he was pointedly disappointed with her. Kate worried she might never see him again. Not until, that is, he brought a bride home to his estate in Clapsforth.

That dark-haired heiress.

Kate stumbled over her partner's foot. "Your pardon." She blinked, struggling to focus on the dance steps.

She pictured Greyson and his bride riding through Clapsforth in an elegant, gold-plated, open barouche. Young girls would sigh with envy, and the villagers would throw flowers. *Her villagers. Her friends.*

Traitors. They would gaze as adoringly as Greyson did at the beautiful heiress with her creamy skin and sparkling diamonds.

No doubt, the young lady would be wearing a stylish bonnet

trimmed with French lace and an ermine-collared coat. They would arrive at Lord Colter's estate. Sally and Mildred, his two housemaids; Abby, his cook; Mr. Foster, the steward; and Edward, who tends Greyson's horses, would all wait in a formal line to greet their new mistress. Lord Colter would sweep his bride up into his arms and carry her over the threshold into his manor house. The two of them would be laughing and smiling and—

No! No! No!

Kate felt like retching. She pressed a hand against her stomach and groaned—an action that elicited a note of concern from her dancing partner. "Are you unwell?"

She nodded. "Um . . . uh, the *incident* earlier seems to be causing me some discomfort."

The gentleman solicitously escorted her off the dance floor. "You are a Trojan, Miss Linnet, and to be greatly admired. However, a reaction of this nature is to be expected. As with all fragile young ladies, you must rest after such strenuous exertion."

Kate bit the inside of her cheek to keep from telling him in rather scathing terms exactly how un-fragile she could be.

"This is absurd." Aunt Honore grumbled all the way out of Almack's assembly rooms.

Nora trailed behind them, waving sweetly at the legion of admirers bidding her a fond farewell. When at last the coach pulled up, Aunt Honore plunked down on the seat with an irritated flourish and glared at Kate. "Such behavior is obscene. You do realize, it's not even close to dawn. There is no reason why we must race home and tuck you in bed at this ridiculously early hour. May I remind you, I have my reputation to consider."

"But, my lady, it cannot be early." Nora's drowsy words sounded as if she'd had too much ratafia to drink. "The clock in the assembly hall said it was nearly three. And I confess, I am dreadfully tired. I can only imagine how poor, dear Katie must feel."

Aunt Honore patted Nora's knee. "Rest, my child. You've had an eventful night. You were an enormous success. With so many gentlemen paying you court, the excitement must have wearied you enormously. There, yes, that's a good girl. Lie your head back and close your eyes."

Kate had never heard Lady Alameda employ such comforting tones. She squinted through the dimly lit coach, straining for a glimpse of this unexpected compassion from her aunt.

However, Aunt Honore turned her face to Kate, and there was nothing comforting about her expression. "You, on the other hand, ought to be ashamed for quitting so soon."

Kate drew back. "But it was Lord *What's-his-name* who *insisted you* take me home because I was overwrought and fatigued."

Aunt Honore's frown deepened.

Kate drew back. "Didn't you hear him? The events on the balcony frayed my delicate nerves." Honore's glare intensified. Kate swallowed. "I'm in dire need of rest."

That much, at least, was true.

Not the part about her nerves, although she did need rest. Truth be told, Kate doubted she would be able to sleep a wink fretting about how badly she'd muddled things with Lord Colter.

"*Delicate nerves.* Balderdash!" Aunt Honore snapped. "I don't believe it—not for an instant." She sulked back against the seat and crossed her arms. "You're not some chicken-hearted mouse. And I daresay you haven't a frayed bone in your body."

Kate sniffed. "My dear Aunt, I assure you, I am quite done in. Moreover, it is not a person's bones that fray—it is their nerves. What's more, there cannot possibly be such a thing as a mouse endowed with a chicken's heart."

"Ha! There, you see! I'm right." Honore leaned forward and shook her finger at Kate. "You have gumption enough to argue with me, which means there's no reason why you can't continue dancing. I'll tell the coachman to turn around."

"No!" Kate lurched up and caught her aunt's arm to stop her from opening the coachman's window. "Please. I beg you. I cannot bear another moment of frivolity tonight." Kate glanced sideways at her sister. "Not only that, but Nora is already asleep."

Honore shook off Kate's hand and sat back, a shrewd ferret-like expression narrowing her eyes. "Very well, Kate. Suppose you tell me the real reason we're leaving Almack's so early?"

"I—I . . ."

Honore didn't wait for Kate to drum up a proper excuse. "You were finally getting some attention from the gentlemen."

Kate looked away, scribbling the tip of her glove against the seat.

"Don't do that," Honore snapped. "The leather oils will soil your gloves. And while we're on the subject of gentlemen suitors, that rather handsome young man you called Lord *What's-his-name* is considered one of this season's most eligible bachelors. Lord Northcote may be a lowly baron now, but he is in line to inherit the title of marquis and, with it, twenty thousand a year. Not, I *think*, a gentleman whose name you should be forgetting."

"I see." Kate clamped her twitching fingers and plunked them in her lap.

"Do you? Your enthusiasm is positively overwhelming." Aunt Honore's sarcasm grated through the night air.

Kate shrugged.

Honore drew in a noisy exasperated breath. "Why not?"

"Because—" Kate caught her lip before blurting the rest of her answer. "I have no interest in giving up my freedom."

The truth.

Despite the dim light of the coach, she blinked, stunned that she'd accidently told such bald truth. But there it was, raw and unvarnished—the thing she hungered for with secret desperation.

"I prefer my freedom." She raised her chin stubbornly. "That's why."

"Ah, I see." Honore said, quietly. "Although, I do wish you had said so sooner. I could've saved £100 on your ballgown."

Startled, Kate shook her head. "No, I—I *wanted* to go to Almack's. I did. And I thank you for your generosity. The gown is lovely, superb, beyond anything I expected."

"Oh, yes. That's right, you *did* want to go. And quite urgently, if I recall correctly." Honore tapped a finger against her cheek. "Remind me again *why* that was? No, wait! Now I have it. You wanted to make certain your poor besotted Lord Colter didn't get snatched up by some lovely heiress. That was the reason, wasn't it?"

Kate sank back against the seat and sighed heavily. "Yes, well, it may be too late for that."

"Too late? Why?"

"Because I'm a bumbling fool."

"Ha!" Aunt Honore snorted. "You'll brook no argument from me."

Kate suddenly felt absurdly bruised and tired and utterly confused. Did she want her freedom or Lord Colter? If only there was a way to have both. Not that she actually had anything resembling freedom now.

She leaned her head back and stared at the dark silk lining the ceiling. If she had an ounce of strength left, she might even cry. But she was beyond tired—she was completely and utterly defeated. Even so, a tear formed in the corner of one eye.

"Phfft!" Honore shoved the toe of her slipper against Kate's shin. "Come now, you're not going to turn missish on me, are you? It isn't your way."

Kate shook her head, banishing her megrims. "No, Aunt."

"Good, because I won't have it. Not from you. Aside from that, you are perfectly right, preferring to keep your independence. It's preferable to marriage in every respect. Think of the tranquility you will have without all the encumbrances of a husband. There'll be no dogs trotting through your house. Men always come with a hound or two. I cannot fathom why, but there it is. They must have one of those flea-bitten creatures following them around. Think of it, my dear, no dogs."

"But we have a dog."

"Well, of course you do. There is a man in the house—your father. You've just proven my point. They come in pairs."

Kate was rather fond of their spaniel. "Papa brought Ralphie home for us girls."

"Rubbish. That's merely what he told you. Now you know the truth." She snapped her fingers. "Do let us return to the salient point. If you remain free, you won't be saddled with taking care of a husband, his hounds, and everyone else in the household. Think, my dear girl. There will never be children hanging onto your skirts or waking you in the middle of the night."

Kate sank back into the shadows so that her aunt wouldn't catch her frowning. True, she'd had her fill of children for the moment, but not forever. Forever was a very long time. She might want one or two of her own someday.

Aunt Honore kept talking.

"—No one fussing every time they bump their elbow or contract some plaguey cold. You won't have a man who wants you to sit by his side and hold his hand while he's sick and dying. And you won't have to worry with burying him when he does die." Melancholy put a sharp edge to her words, and it reminded Kate that her aunt was a widow. How hard that must have been for Honore. Rumor has it that Francisco de Alameda had been the love of her life, the only man she would ever deign to marry.

Kate considered how she would cope with Greyson dying. The thought made her stomach surge as if a cannon ball had dropped into it. I idea of him dying without her there to hold his hand made her soul shrink into a dark cocoon.

She opened her mouth to protest but Honore kept rattling

on.

"Think of it, dear. No husband to shout at you if you spend too much on a perfectly delightful bonnet. No one grumbling about his investments failing in the market or complaining about the latest irksome war. You won't have anyone inflicting you with troublesome relatives or annoying friends. Yes, Katie, my girl, freedom is the wisest choice."

"Is it?" Kate murmured, now utterly convinced the opposite must be true.

"Undoubtedly," Honore answered softly, gazing out of the window at the black emptiness of London at night. "'Tis all for the best."

Kate peered through the dimly lit coach at her aunt. In that shadowy light, Honore looked small and lost. And alone. Dreadfully alone.

And if one word of what Honore said was true, why did the woman keep inviting nieces and nephews to shelter under her wings?

Lies.

All of it lies.

Chapter 18
Tilly's Last Stand

IT WAS THREE forty-five in the morning by the time Kate shed her clothes and readied herself for bed. When she finally crawled under the covers, Tilly rolled over and blinked her eyes open. "Did you mend things with Lord Colter?"

"Go back to sleep."

"That means no."

"It means . . ." Kate paused, hunting for a suitable answer. "It's no concern of yours."

"It is, too, my concern." Tilly thumped the mattress and sat up. "I won't let you marry anyone else and move a thousand miles away."

"Don't be absurd. No place in Britain is a thousand miles away. Aside from that you have no say in the matter. Now, hush and go back to sleep."

"I do have a say." She crossed her arms. "And I won't allow

it."

Kate was too muddled to do battle with Tilly. She rolled over, stiffened her back against her militant sister, yanked the covers over her shoulder, and pretended to sleep. She had no idea how long Tilly sat there sulking. Because pretending to sleep produced unexpected results, Kate sank into inescapable nightmarish dreams—rattling along in Greyson's galloping carriage only to be tossed out by the dark-haired heiress. The next moment she found herself on her hands and knees in the dirt, being used as a step stool for the heiress to climb down into Greyson's waiting arms.

With each fitful start, Kate awakened fuzzily only to drift back into that murky, nocturnal hell of her own making. Hours later, while batting at the covers, she muttered in her sleep, "No. No—No!" She would not surrender—except dark hair and rich silks coiled snake-like around her neck, stealing her life. Kate fought to escape her enemy's stranglehold, slapping and kicking the vicious terrors away. But instead of regaining Greyson's waiting embrace, he vanished, and an obnoxious pillar of sunlight smacked her in the face.

Only a bad dream.

A dozen horrid dreams.

Yet, the night terrors had shown her the truth—it was not freedom she was afraid of losing. It was Greyson. And she needed to fight for what she wanted. Kate blinked at the sunlight slicing into her eyes.

"Shut the curtains," she groaned and flopped over.

No one answered.

She pulled a pillow over her head. "Have mercy, Tilly. Close the curtains."

Still no answer.

Exasperated, Kate flung the pillow aside and sat up. The room was empty. She squinted at the clock—half-past two.

Great green polliwogs! She'd nearly slept the day away. That would not do! Not when she had so much to accomplish. Broken fences to mend. Heiresses to slay. Not that she would actually slay that dratted dark-haired beauty, but neither would she let Miss *Whatever-her-name-is* sink her evil claws into Greyson. For she must surely be evil. After the nightmares Kate had, could there be any doubt about the woman's character?

She no sooner swung her feet over the side of the bed when the door flew open and Sadie burst in. "There's a line! Get up. Hurry! You'll never believe it."

"Do stop shouting, dearest. My head is throbbing."

Sadie tugged on her arm. "But Katie. There's a line down the street. Come to the window and see for yourself."

Katie extracted herself from her sister's grip. "What are you going on about? A line of what?"

"Gentlemen." Sadie ran to the window, raised the sash, and pointed. "Look! Have you ever seen anything like it?"

Kate didn't move. Was this another awful dream? If she went to the window, her sister might shove her out, she'd be dashed to pieces in the street, and the heiress's carriage would roll over her lifeless limbs. Kate squeezed her eyes shut against the gruesome image.

"Come away from there, Sadie." Kate massaged her aching forehead, still adjusting to the bright light. "Stop hanging out the window like a yokel. It isn't done."

"But you have to see this." Sadie stayed there and waved her hand for Kate to come and see. "They're lined up to call on Nora, and some might even be here for you, too. Aunt Honore won't let them in the house. Not until the stroke of three. She says it is indecent of them to call any earlier than that."

"Callers?"

"That's what I've been trying to tell you."

Kate got up, stubbed her toe against the oak night table, and hopped the rest of the way to the window. She stood to the side and inched back the curtain. A line of men in top hats stretched down the street.

"Good gracious!" She let go of the curtain and flattened herself against the wall. "What is happening?"

"Callers. I told you—"

"Yes, obviously. But why?"

"Well, I suppose because Nora is attractive. Some people say charming and—"

"You don't understand. It is one thing to be beautiful or even charming. Quite another to draw a crowd like that. There has to be an explanation . . ." She thumped her head back against the wall. "*Aunt Honore.*" Her wicked scheming aunt had to be behind this absurd battalion of callers. It was the only explanation. "*Clothes!* Help me find some clothes."

Eight minutes later, Kate was garbed in a serviceable morning gown, including all of the appropriate undergarments and, *luckily*, both of her stockings matched. She yanked on her sturdiest kid slippers and glanced up at Sadie. "Where's Tilly? I would've thought she'd be trailing behind you."

"Haven't seen her all morning."

"Not at all?"

Sadie shook her head while pinching up one of Kate's wayward, blonde locks. "We'd better do something about your hair. It's a fright. Looks like burnt apple strudel."

Kate grimaced and handed Sadie the hairbrush. "Careful. You'll turn my head with such compliments."

It took another five and a half minutes to brush out her hair and wind it into a tight bun. "It will do," Kate pronounced.

Sadie sniffed disdainfully and set down the brush. "I doubt Lady Jersey would think so."

Kate headed out of the bedroom. "I intend to have a word with our wayward aunt. You go find your sister."

"Ohhh, but I want to hear this—"

"Go find Tilly!" Kate pointed from the top of the stairs. "Now."

Sadie's face puckered into a red pout. "I never get to do anything fun. I didn't get to go to Almack's, and now you won't even let me hear you argue with our aunt." She stamped her foot but turned and, mumbling something rude, left to do as she was told.

Kate didn't have time to correct Sadie. Her morning was starting out almost as annoying as her unrestful night. She marched down the stairs rehearsing the stern speech she planned to deliver to Aunt Honore.

When she arrived in the sitting room, she stopped short. Aunt Honore and a maid were busy arranging Nora in the center of the sofa, tilting her sister's chin and positioning her shoulders. Honore tapped her cheek, surveying their handiwork. "One more flower in her hair, I think."

The maid tucked a pale primrose into Nora's perfectly coiffed curls. Poised on the cushions, Nora wore the most angelic, white silk gown Kate had ever seen. It had a diaphanous, white organza overdress artfully trimmed with real flowers in various shades of pink. The combination seemed both seductive yet sublimely innocent. "Spread her skirts a little. Expose a tiny bit more of her ankles. Yes, that's it."

Cairn shifted restlessly near the door. "M'lady, the hour is upon us."

"Not just yet, Cairn. Make them wait a few more minutes."

"I fear a riot may erupt. The lads tell me a dozen of the gentlemen have already resorted to fisticuffs."

"Did they now?" Honore chuckled. "Perfect. Everything is just as it should be."

Kate had heard enough. She strode forward. "What is the meaning of all this? Why are gentlemen lined up around the block? And why are they fighting?"

Lady Alameda gestured imperiously at the princess serenely enthroned on the sofa. "Need you ask? Your sister is the catch of the season. A work of art, is she not?"

Nora blushed a delicate pink and stared down at her hands folded gracefully in her lap.

Kate crossed her arms with considerable irritation. "Fiddlesticks!"

"Hush, my dear." Honore laid a finger on her lips and shook her head. "You know how your father feels about strong language."

Kate suppressed a growl. "I was not born yesterday, Aunt.

Charm and beauty count for very little in London's high society."

"Is that so? Humph. Explains why you take so little care with your appearance. Really dear, I do wish you would try a little har—"

"Nonsense! You have said something to entice these gentlemen here. You must have. You know perfectly well that Nora does not have a large enough dowry to attract this many suitors. Even if Papa gives her my portion, he cannot settle more than £300 on her. And we both know that is not nearly enough to attract a crowd of this size."

Honore wrinkled her nose briefly. "Only 300? Hhmm, I would've thought he could afford a trifle more than that."

"Then you would've been mistaken. I ask again, what have you told these people?"

"*These* people? Nothing. Not a blessed thing." She threw up her hands. But when Kate continued to glare severely at her, Lady Alameda shrugged. "Oh, very well. I vaguely recall mentioning something to Lady Blatherstone. It is not my fault the woman is a shameful gossip. And I *may* have miscalculated by a zero or two. But what does it matter?" Honore spun on her heel and smiled at Nora, who despite this unsettling intelligence still sat as serene and unruffled as a morning dove.

Honore chuckled lightly and added, "Everyone assumes I will leave my money to *someone*. Why shouldn't it be Nora?"

"Your heir?" Kate sputtered. "You put it about that Nora was your heir? But cousin Marcus is your son by marriage—surely, he stands to inherit. Fiona told me as much."

"Phfft! What can Fiona know about it?" Honore's voice leapt up in pitch. "Haven't seen her in months. She's too busy pushing out brats for Lord Somebody-or-other. And I'll have you know, who I leave my inheritance to is my business and no one else's. It might very well be Nora. Or for that matter, even *you*—my stubborn mule-headed girl."

"Stubborn and mule-headed mean the same—*oh, never mind!* We both know you would never choose me." Kate bristled at her aunt's flippant smirk. "More importantly, putting that sort of rumor about in society is not only dishonest, it is also misleading and—

Honore raised her finger, stopping Kate's tirade. "Doesn't *misleading* mean the same thing as *dishonest*?" At Kate's stern frown, Honore tilted her nose higher. "Well, you're the one who's always so particular about words."

"Spreading false rumors is not only dishonest, it is also dangerous. Have you forgotten Fiona was nearly murdered because of just such a lie?"

"Are you calling me a liar?" Aunt Honore snorted. "How dare you—"

"Katie. Katie!" Sadie raced into the room, yelling as if the house were on fire. "She's missing! Tilly's nowhere to be found. None of the servants have seen her."

"What?" Kate grasped her sister's shoulders. "You looked everywhere? The closets? The kitchens?"

Sadie nodded and leaned over to catch her breath. "Gone."

Kate's hands clenched into desperate knots. Her heart galloped as if she'd plunged over a cliff. Her baby sister was missing. She restrained a screech threatening to erupt and calmly asked, "When did you see her last?"

"Breakfast."

Kate turned to Honore. "Aunt?"

"Yes, yes, I saw her at breakfast, too. The little scamp was pestering me for Lord Colter's address."

Greyson's address. Kate cringed, adding up what this meant—Tilly might be wandering the streets of London in search of Lord Colter. She choked out the next few words. "And did you tell her?"

"No!" Honore threw up her hands. "I told her to stop fussing at me and that the coachman was the only one who knew Lord Colter's direction."

"The coachman!" Kate whirled to Sadie. "Did you try the stables?"

Sadie, her eyes widening, shook her head.

Nora sprang from the sofa. "We'd better check."

"Sit back down," Aunt Honore scolded. "You have an army of callers waiting for you."

Nora shook her head, and one of her pale pink primroses went flying. "My sisters come first!" she said, with more force than Kate had ever heard from Nora. "Katie, what shall we do?"

"Don't be ridiculous," Honore scoffed. "You're making much ado about nothing. The child will be fine."

"You don't know that," Kate protested. "We've all heard stories about how treacherous a place London is for innocent young girls."

Honore harumphed. "It's not as if she'll wander into those parts of London. I daresay the little scamp has more sense than all three of you put together."

Aunt Honore may as well have been singing to the walls. Nora and Sadie kept their gazes fixed on Kate, awaiting her orders. They needed clear-headed guidance. She swallowed and drew in a deep breath, pleading for wisdom. Then, as if an ocean breeze blew away the morning fog, Kate knew what they ought to do.

She turned to Nora. "I know this will be difficult, but I must ask you to stay here—"

"But I want to help."

"I know, darling, and you shall." She rested a comforting hand on Nora's shoulder. "We need you to invite all of your gentlemen callers into the sitting room. And you know how affecting it is when you weep." Kate brushed a curl back from Nora's cheek. "You must do so today. Let them know how terribly grieved you are by your baby sister's disappearance. Explain that this very morning she innocently wandered off into the environs of London, and we know not where. Think of it, dearest, our Tilly is all alone. Lost on the treacherous streets of London—a helpless little girl."

"Helpless. Phfft! Not that one." Aunt Honore batted away Kate's words and crossed her arms. "She may be a child, but she's not helpless. Not her. A lion in lamb's wool, that one."

Kate ignored Lady Alameda's abused metaphor and yet noted Honore's agitation—her aunt's stiff posture and bouncing impatient leg. Her aunt appeared to be more concerned than she let on.

Kate turned away and continued instructing Nora. "Let the gentlemen know that until Tilly is found, you cannot possibly entertain guests. Tell them you are so grieved that you must take to your bed and weep."

Nora nodded. Her eyes widened and began to water. Kate

could scarcely keep her own from welling up in response, but she needed to remain strong.

"Yes. That's it. Good," Kate sniffed. "Very good." She patted Nora's shoulder. "That ought to spur at least some of the gentlemen into action. We need all the help we can get in our search. Give them a description. And here—pass my locket among them. The likeness is close enough." Taking one last glimpse at the miniature painting of her little Tilly, Kate unlatched it from around her neck and handed Nora the locket. "Sadie and I will speak with the coachman and do our best to find her." She kissed Nora's damp cheek. "After you dismiss your callers, please remain at hand in case Tilly comes home or one of the gentlemen finds her. One of us ought to be here."

Aunt Honore headed for the door right behind Kate and Sadie. "Do as the young lady asks, Cairn. Allow in that mob of suitors. Squeeze them all in however you must. I'll return as soon as I have dispatched a few notes."

Notes?

Kate wondered if her aunt might be sending for a Bow Street Runner or one of the shadowy men that sometimes came or went so covertly from her study. Kate could not wait for runners or spies. She had to find Tilly now.

They found the coachman inspecting fittings on one of the coach wheels. He stood and brushed off his hands. "Aye, the young lady came around asking questions." He refused to meet Kate's intense gaze and reluctantly admitted giving Lord Colter's direction to Tilly.

Kate groaned.

"She said your aunt sent her, but I had me doubts." The

coachman turned a worried expression on Kate and dug the toe of his boot into the dirt. "I should've listened to me conscience. Leastwise, I warned her it t'ain't safe for a youngster to go traipsin' about unaccompanied."

"I doubt she listened." Sadie heaved a sigh.

"'S'pect you'd be right." The coachman rubbed at his forehead. "The little mite lifted her chin as if I were a right scoundrel to even suggest such a thing. '*I'm well aware of what is proper and what is not*, says she. *Good day to you, sir.*' Your young miss marched away with her back quite stiff. Pardon me for saying so."

Kate cringed. "I apologize for my sister's rude behavior, but I suspect the child is doing precisely what you advised her not to do. In which case, she could lose her way or find herself in all manner of danger. If we hurry, there's a chance we might catch up to her—that is, if you would please drive us to Lord Colter's lodgings?"

"Right away, miss." He pulled on his forelock. "I'll hitch up the chaise—that'll be faster. We'll be on our way in a trice."

He shouted for the stable lads, who brought out a large bay and hooked him into the traces. As soon as the coachman helped Kate and Sadie into the buggy, he tapped his whip and they bowled onto the streets of Mayfair.

"This is just like Tilly," Sadie slapped the leather seat between them. "The little fool. What makes her think she can take matters into her own hands as if she rules the world?" Sadie didn't really expect an answer to her question. She rapped Kate's leg angrily. "She gets that from you, you know."

Kate stifled the lump welling up in her throat. "I know." She didn't have the heart to argue. Sadie was right. This was Kate's fault. Any thoughts she may have had about wanting her freedom or thinking her sisters were an unfair burden flew out of her mind like useless moths. The only thing that mattered now was finding her little Tilly.

"I am sorry." Kate grabbed Sadie's hand and gripped it for support. "But right now, Tilly could be anywhere. Watch for her on your side of the street, and I will search mine."

Kate strained forward, studying the people on the walk, hunting for her sister's familiar shape and size, ignoring the indignant stares of passersby. One matron, in particular, frowned disapprovingly, and Kate realized she'd dashed out of the house without a bonnet. She must look like a gawking hayseed. But what did it matter? Her little sister was in danger.

_Chapter 19
All That Glowers is Not Gloomy

NO SIGN OF TILLY.

Not until Kate spotted a girl in the crowd who looked Tilly's height and build. "Stop!" she shouted. Their coachman swerved, pulled up short, and nearly caused a collision with another carriage. Kate leapt out to investigate, but when she grasped the girl's shoulder, her quarry turned out to be a very short and startled lady.

She apologized, but the lady scurried away fearfully, and Kate returned disheartened to the chaise.

Two blocks later, the rig stopped in a more orderly manner in front of Lord Colter's narrow rented townhouse. Kate and Sadie solemnly climbed out and approached the door. "Please, please, please," Sadie muttered as Kate raised her hand to the knocker.

She, too, found herself praying the door would open and Tilly would be standing hand in hand with Lord Colter. She knew he would be glowering and peeved at her. After her behavior at Almack's, he had a right to be. But if Tilly stood beside him, she wouldn't mind if he frowned at all.

Taking a deep breath, Kate rapped firmly. Behind the wooden barrier, she heard, "Who in blazes can that be?" She'd know Greyson's voice anywhere. But today, just as she'd anticipated, his ordinarily soothing baritone did, indeed, sound uncharacteristically irritated. "Never mind, Stevens. Keep chiseling that ice. I'll see to it."

Swallowing a lump of anxiety, Kate fixed her gaze midway up the door, crossing her fingers and hoping to see Tilly standing next to him. The brusque thump of his stride as he approached diminished her optimism considerably.

The door swung open.

No Tilly.

"Kate!" He sounded shocked.

Her gaze drifted from where Tilly was *not* standing up to Greyson's widened eyes—one of which was puffy, swollen, and red. And his lip was cut.

Kate's mouth opened in alarm, but before she could utter a word, Sadie blurted, "What happened to you?"

Greyson only mumbled in response. His beautiful kissable mouth had a swollen split lip. There was blood dribbling onto his chin and red splatters strewn across his shirt.

"You're bleeding!" Kate finally found words. *Obvious*

words. She groaned inwardly, yet there they were, tripping childishly out of her mouth. "There's blood on your—" She intended to say chin, but too late realized she was staring too long at his lips.

"I'm well aware." He didn't even look at her.

She snapped to her senses, yanked a handkerchief from her pocket, and reached up to dab at his injured mouth. He arrested her hands mid-reach and held them hostage in front of him. "Kate—stop. My man will attend to it. What are you doing here? It isn't proper. These are gentleman's quarters. A young lady shouldn't—"

"We had to come." Sadie stamped her foot. "Tilly is missing!"

"What?!" Greyson let go of Kate's hands. "When? How? What is being done?"

All the right questions. Kate wanted to collapse into his arms. Instead, spider-thin threads of dignity held her together. "We thought she might have come here."

"Here?" He gawked. "Why would Tilly come here?"

"She, um . . ." Heat raced into Kate's cheeks, but there was no help for it. Only the truth would do. "She wanted to repair matters between you and me."

"Stevens!" He hollered into the next room. "Did a child call while I was out? A young girl?"

The steady chunking and chiseling of ice halted. "No, m'lord. I'm afraid not." His servant approached, carrying a bulging cloth bag. Stevens stared down his nose at Kate and Sadie as if they were gutter vermin the cat had dragged in.

"However, m'lord, I do believe I've chipped enough ice for your eye. Shall I apply it for you?"

"No, I can manage." Greyson pressed the muslin bag against his puffy red eye, and turned back to Kate. His good eye peered at her quite sternly. "When did you see Tilly last? The exact time."

Sadie answered for them. "Breakfast."

Kate noticed his knuckles were a reddish-purple color, and there were sizeable rips in Greyson's shirt and sleeve. Beneath the torn cloth, she spied another plum-colored welt the size of a fist.

She drew in a sharp breath. "Good heavens! You've been in a fight? What happened? Were you set upon by a band of thieves?"

It must've been a gang of thugs because no one man could've done this much damage—not to Greyson.

"Not thieves," he grumbled, wincing as he adjusted the ice. "Worse."

"Worse?" She could not stop the shrill octave to which her voice jumped. "What, then? Did a carriage hit you?" *He could've been killed.* Awaiting his answer, her breath stuttered and hammered her chest in short frantic bursts. "Greyson?"

"Calm yourself. Nothing so dire. If you must know, it was a half-dozen overeager lords outside your aunt's townhouse."

"What?" He was not making sense.

He shrugged, which prompted a wince. "Apparently, the gentlemen didn't think I had a right to circumvent their line."

"*That* fight . . ." Kate stepped back, frowning and blinking away her disbelief. "That was you?"

Sadie snickered. "Well done, you."

Kate swatted her sister's arm. "It is not well done. *And* it certainly is not a laughing matter." She turned back to him. "Not at all. Why would you do such a thing?"

He lowered the ice pack and leaned down till they were almost nose to nose. "You didn't think I was going to let Lord Northcote get the jump on me, did you?"

"The *jump on you?* Lord Northcote?" Kate edged back, trying to make sense of his words. "You intend to court Nora?" Her heart sank. "Surely, you didn't fall for that rumor about her inheritance. It's all a hum. Aunt Honore isn't really going to leave her estate to Nora."

Greyson put the ice back on his eye. "Have your wits gone begging? I wasn't there for her. Not Nora. *You.*"

Kate's breathing stopped, and her heart did a silly twirl.

Me?

Greyson came to call on me.

He'd tried to fight his way to the front of the line. *Those dreadful bruises were earned on my account.* It was awful, yet she couldn't help smiling.

Then Greyson turned his one-eyed, stern frown on her again. "Tilly—if she's not here, where else might she have gone?"

All the delight that had just filled her heart plunked out and plummeted through the floorboards. *Where else?* "This is the only place. She was intent on settling matters with you. If she didn't arrive here, it must mean she's . . . she's . . ." Kate couldn't bring herself to say it.

"Lost," Sadie supplied.

"We'll find her." Greyson set the ice bag in a bowl on the side table. "Ferguson, call round for my horse!"

Kate shook her head. "No need. We have a chaise waiting out front."

"Good. My coat." Lord Colter snapped his fingers. "Quickly, man." Coat supplied, the three of them rushed out to the waiting gig.

The chaise, being a smaller conveyance, meant Sadie must sit atop Kate's lap. "Where to, miss?" the coachman asked.

Where? Kate rubbed the tight-knit furrow between her brows and turned to Greyson. His concern mirrored hers, but he straightened, and his features hardened into stern determination. "We'll start by scouring the streets between my lodgings and Lady Alameda's townhouse."

A slap of the reins, and they set off at a slow pace. They went up and down the streets of Mayfair, leaning out in search of anyone resembling little lost Tilly, ignoring the disapproving stares of people strolling along the walkways.

Sadie thought she saw her and eagerly pointed, "Tilly!"

At Sadie's raucous shout, the girl turned to look in their direction. Instead of Tilly's fair hair, the bonnet had hidden brunette hair. Sadie ducked back into the confines of the chaise, and their hunt continued. An hour and a half later, they had covered all the streets and byways between the two abodes and expanded their search to include a substantial radius.

"I'm hungry," Sadie moaned.

"How can you think of food at a time like this?" Kate's stomach had long since tied itself into a fretful knot.

"Don't blame me. I'm not thinking of food. It's my stomach what's thinking of it." Sadie shifted on Kate's lap, just enough that some of the feeling returned to Kate's leg in a rush of pins and needles.

Kate grimaced.

"Would you like me to take her?" Greyson offered.

"It wouldn't be proper." Kate sighed and tried to ease more of Sadie's weight onto her other leg.

"It wouldn't be *improper* if he were my brother-in-law. This whole mess is your fault. Tilly would never have run away if you'd simply agreed to marry Lord Colter like you were supposed to do." Sadie crossed her arms and bounced intentionally, making Kate wince as prickles spiked through her leg. Sadie dug an elbow into Kate's ribs, letting loose more of her frustration. "I'm not just hungry. I'm squished to pieces in this tiny carriage, and that's all your fault, too. If you would've—"

"Enough, Sadie!" Greyson used a commanding tone that startled both girls. "Kate has sacrificed everything for you and your sisters. You will speak to her with the respect she deserves."

The respect she deserves.

Kate stared at Greyson. She stopped hearing the clank of

the buggy wheels, the clatter of horse hooves. The world receded into a thick irrelevant fog. Floodgates inside her burst open, and a torrent of long-forgotten hope overflowed, rushing into the cracked, dry wounds of her soul.

Greyson understood.

He knew the girl inside her—the person she'd given up on so she could take care of her family. Had he always seen the real her? In that moment, Kate realized no one else on God's green earth would ever know her as deeply as he did.

She didn't know she was crying until hot tears stung her cheeks. Embarrassed, she swiped them away.

"Oh." Sadie leaned in softly and hugged her. "I'm sorry, Katie. I didn't mean it." She rested her forehead against Kate's. "Let's keep looking for Tilly. I'll ignore my stomach."

As if on cue, Sadie's belly made a rather loud complaint of its own.

Kate exchanged a half-hearted smile with Greyson as she returned Sadie's hug. "Perhaps we ought to return you to Lady Alameda's house. Anyway, there's a chance Tilly may have turned up by now. If she hasn't, you can wait there with Nora while Lord Colter and I continue searching.

Greyson nodded and tapped the coachman on the shoulder. "To Lady Alameda's, with haste, my good man."

"Right-o, m'lord." Their driver clucked to his horse, and the eager bay took off at a brisk trot.

Aunt Honore's butler opened the door, and Nora stood right behind him, leaning up to see over his shoulder, anxiously clutching her skirts. "Any sign of her?"

Kate shook her head. "Have you heard anything?"

"No." Nora's gaze drooped to the marble tile. "Nothing."

Kate exhaled loudly. "Never mind. We will keep searching. But Sadie is hungry. If you would, please—"

"Certainly." Nora put her arm around Sadie and took her off to find something to eat.

Tilly is lost.

Kate turned her distress on the butler, entreating him as if Nora must've been mistaken. "Perhaps my aunt received word of the child's whereabouts?"

"No, miss. I'm afraid not." Cairn bowed and turned away, disappearing down a corridor.

Kate's shoulders bowed as she slumped onto a bench in the entry hall. She lowered her head into her hands. "I've lost her," she groaned. "I've heard what happens to a young girl on her own in the city. I can't bear to think of it." She shook her head, still hiding her face in her hands. "How will I tell Papa? If anything happens to her, I'll—I'll—"

"We will find her." Greyson squatted in front of Kate and tucked some loose strands of hair behind her ear. "She's bound to be nearby, not in the heart of London where those things happen. We'll keep hunting until we find her. And we might have better luck if we search on foot. After all, how far can a ten-year-old wander?"

A fair distance.

However . . . Kate reconsidered and looked up. "You have a point. When she was little, Tilly had a habit of hiding when frightened. If she were to grasp the enormity of London and realize she is hopelessly lost, she might curl up in some dark nook or a crevice between the houses." Kate revived, clutching at the thin strand of hope. "And, like Sadie, she'll be getting hungry and trying to figure out how to get food."

"Right. I noticed many of these larger townhouses have gardens in the back. She might venture out for an apple or carrot." He regarded Kate with the same earnest hope she felt.

"Yes! Gardens and fruit trees." Optimism fluttered its tiny wings inside her. "She might've climbed into a tree. From the coach, we'd never have spotted her tucked up in the branches. We should check alleyways and coaching house drives."

Thank you, her heart sang, and she smiled into his hopeful face. "Oh, Greyson, your poor eye. It's turning purple." She reached for his cheek and delicately smoothed her fingers over the swelling. "And your lip."

"I see you two have reconciled your differences."

Kate hadn't heard her aunt approach. With a groan, she withdrew her fingers from his face. Greyson stood abruptly and cleared his throat. "We were just, uh, considering where the child might be. I think perhaps we ought to search for her on foot."

"Hhmm." Aunt Honore sounded skeptical. "Well then, don't let me stop you."

Kate tilted her head, confused by her aunt's response. "Surely you will want to come with us and help?"

"Will I?" Honore pressed a hand over her breast. "Me? Out there? Rooting around back alleys like a common vagabond? I think not." Her hand dropped away and her nose lifted substantially. "Not I. One hires Bow Street Runners for that sort of thing. Aside from that, it's a fool's errand. I'm not worried in the least. The child will turn up. They always do. I ran away a few times myself. I'm quite certain your sister is out there—" She whisked her hand through the air encompassing all of London. "—having a marvelous adventure."

Are you mad?

A marvelous adventure?

"Tilly is lost. Alone! She's bound to be terribly frightened." Kate shot to her feet, bristling at her aunt's indifference. "Come, Lord Colter." She took his waiting arm. "Let us be off." She glared hard at her aunt, but Honore seemed impervious to shame and completely lacking in even an iota of proper concern for Tilly's welfare.

Kate marched down the street, seething. "How can she be so callous? So uncaring? I swear, the woman is as mad as a hatter. Papa was right. We never should have trusted my sisters with her."

"It was mentioned," Greyson muttered. Two blocks later, he reined in her galloping gait. "If we're to hunt for Tilly in those back alleys and dark crevices you mentioned, you may want to slow down."

"You're right." She stopped and her shoulders sagged. "It's just that my aunt can be so infuriating at times."

"Just so." He agreed, frowning, except his attention diverted to a stairwell beside them. He peered intently into the dark depths leading to a below-ground-level servants' entrance. "And after we find your sister . . ."

"Yes?"

He swung around the railing and went down the first few steps. "She's not here," he exhaled his disappointment and hurried out. "After we find her . . ."

"Yes?" She walked beside him, keeping a close watch on his face.

He stopped abruptly, turned, and grasped her shoulders. "After all this is over, and when Tilly is safely returned to us, I want . . ."

He seemed reluctant to spit it out, so Kate blurted the first inane thing that popped into her mind. "You want a dog?"

"A dog?" His brows shot up, and the unswollen side of his mouth curled skeptically as if he thought maybe she'd hit her head.

"Aunt Honore says every man wants a dog." *There. That explains it.*

"Well, yes, I suppose she has a point. But I want more than that, Kate. I want a great many things."

"Money?"

He winced. "Yes. Naturally, I want my estate to produce more than it is—the crops and livestock to fare better." He sighed. "The tenants need new roofs. If only my sheep would reproduce faster—"

"I've mentioned before, you might want to consider raising pigs."

He drew in an irritated breath. "And as I've told you before, I don't like pigs."

"You eat bacon." She couldn't leave it be—but at least she said it very quietly.

"Yes, but I don't like pigs. They're selfish, stubborn, and they'll eat anything, including their own young."

She wrinkled her nose. "True, but most people are quite fond of ham. Ergo, you'd make more money."

He frowned impatiently. "Money is beside the point."

"Very well. If not money, what else do you want, aside from dogs?"

"Sunday dinners. Geese in the yard. Cats in the barn. Children. All of it. And yes, I know, children have runny noses. They track mud all over the house, they get fussy, and they keep one up all night, and—"

And . . .

Her mind raced through a litany of horrors. "They get sick. *You* might get sick." It flew out of her mouth in a strangled gust.

"Well, I suppose they do . . ." He froze midsentence, gaping at her as if she'd suddenly confessed her love. It flitted across his features and blew away in a puff of air. "Phfft," he smirked. "I'm not the sickly sort."

Maybe not. Yet . . .

Aunt Honore's dismal soliloquy about holding her dying husband's hand taunted Kate.

People *did* die.

All too often.

Her mother had died, and left Kate with a baby to raise.

Kate toyed with the torn button on his jacket. "Except you might. No one is immune to getting ill."

"Yes, there is that. Very well." He brushed a finger across her cheek as if he understood her unspoken worries. "I suppose anything is possible." The tenderness in his voice melted over her heart like warm chocolate. "For that matter, my darling girl, *you* might get sick."

"No." She flashed up at him. "I wouldn't. I won't! I would never leave you to care for everything on your own."

"I know. I know." He clasped her shoulders to calm her. "But if ever you did, Kate, I would want to be there at your bedside, watching over you. But more than that, someday I want to hear our children's laughter down the hall. And yours, Kate. I want to hear your laughter. I want a hundred things. I want picnics, kite flying, egg gathering, and to go fishing in the river with my sons—"

"What about our daughters? *Daughters* can fish, too."

"Yes, of course! If you wish it, I'll teach them to fish—*our* daughters, *our* sons, your sisters. All of them." He grinned. "And I've no doubt, when they're older, every one of them will try our patience, break our hearts, and at other times they'll shower us with joy. Life is full of troublesome storms mixed with gloriously happy moments."

She stared at his shining face, at his bruised eye, his split lip, and bloody shirt—the most beautiful man she'd ever seen.

What a fearful fool she'd been.

Greyson held her shoulders tighter and kept talking when

all she wanted to do was kiss him. "Kate, my darling, that's what love is. When storm winds blow their hardest, it is the stone wall behind which we hide. It keeps us afloat when floodwaters rise. And in the same way, when joy overflows our souls, love is the trumpet that sings in our hearts and teaches our feet to dance. Do you see?"

She did.

She did see. For the first time, Kate understood with perfect clarity. Tears blurred her vision, but she saw far beyond his jumbled lists and heartfelt metaphors—miles into the future, dozens of years hence. Her life opened out before her like a peddler's pack brimming with wares, both tarnished and gleaming. And what she saw was that the burdens she carried today, and those she would carry tomorrow, would turn out to be her greatest treasures.

He kissed her cheek, tears and all. "What matters is that we face whatever comes *together*."

"Together," she murmured.

"Yes." He hugged her. "More than anything else, that's what I want. I love you, Kate. I have since we were children. After your mother died, I saw how you took care of your sisters and looked after your father. I watched you give up the frivolity and silliness that consumed the other girls in our village. While they were picking out ribbons for themselves, you were carefully selecting ribbons for Nora or Sadie. While other girls were giggling and sampling sweets at the bake shop, you were wiping Tilly's chin and giving Sadie a half-pence to buy rolls. My heart ached, wishing for some way to help. Then there was that day sledding on the hill. Do you remember?"

Their first kiss?

How could she ever forget?

He didn't wait for her reply. "After most of their friends left, Sadie complained of the cold, and Nora offered to take both of the younger girls home. They left along with everyone else. You stood at the top of that hill holding your rickety, old sled and dared, just for a moment, to be a girl yourself."

Kate caught her lip, remembering flying down the hill and that exhilarating feeling of freedom.

He laughed and shook his head. "You should've seen your face, Katie. Despite gray skies and the cold, you glowed with delight. You let out a whoop and dove onto the sled, sliding down the hill so fast I thought for certain you'd end up in the river. I broke into a sprint, but you veered off into the trees. And then . . ." His expression softened and his cheeks flushed.

"You kissed me."

"I did." The corner of his mouth twisted upward. "That's when I knew I wanted to be with you always, through tumbles and troubles, laughter and kisses—through it all. Oh Kate, say you'll spend the rest of your life with me."

Silent sobs racked Kate's shoulders, and if he had not been holding her, she might've collapsed. If she opened her mouth, she was afraid her emotions would rush out in an incoherent gurgle. And there might be more tears, the horridly loud kind, the kind that twisted up one's face in a most hideous manner.

Kate was not the crying sort, yet today she'd become a

veritable watering pot. She turned away, wiping at her eyes. Through the watery mess, she thought she spied Tilly strolling up the walk towards them.

Impossible.

Kate gasped and hastily wiped her eyes.

"What is it!?" Greyson grabbed her shoulders again. "What's wrong?"

Chapter 20
The Girl and the Tiger

KATE PULLED OUT of Greyson's embrace and turned back to the blurry form of her sister. "Tilly?"

Greyson saw it, too. "What in blazes—"

Kate's vision cleared completely.

It is Tilly!

It was Tilly. Her very own little Tilly strolling along licking a lollipop, as nonchalant as a puppy in the park. Tilly, not looking ragged and forlorn. Not frightened and lost. Not starving. Tilly, indulging in a sweet—one she must have stolen because the child had no pin money of her own.

Kate's tears withered into salty dust. Surprise evaporated into something else. Something smoldering and dangerous. Kate's back stiffened. Her fingers curled tight. "Brat! You little wretch. How could you?"

Tilly looked up from her sweet on a stick and grinned. "Good day, Katie!" She waved as carefree and innocent as the birds flitting in the breeze above them.

Good day?

It has been a perfectly dreadful day.

Well, except for when Greyson helped me see that my burdens are my greatest treasures in life. And I would've kissed him, except you—

Tilly raised the sweet. "Look what I got."

"Look what I *have*," Kate corrected out of habit, standing stiff as a fence post in the middle of the sidewalk.

"It's a lollipop." Tilly babbled on, oblivious of the fact that she'd been horribly lost and might've spent the night in a rat-infested gutter somewhere, or worse. "Isn't it marvelous?" She held it up and twirled it in her fingers. She squinted at their silent nonreaction, and must've guessed the problem was her lack of proper manners, as was often the case, so Tilly curtsied. "Pleased to see you, Lord Colter. Did my sister do that to your eye?"

"No. I, uh—"

"Then why are you crying, Katie? Did he say something mean to you?" Tilly turned a stern glare on Greyson.

"No!" He stepped back. "Quite the contrary. We've been making amends."

"Oh? Well, that's all right then. Splendid news. Carry on." Tilly grinned and slurped on her sweet. "Aunt Honore told me to stop sticking my nose into adult matters. She said that if I wanted the two of you to fall back in love, I needed to stand aside, mind my own business, and do exactly as she said." Tilly shook her head, ringlets bouncing. "Our aunt appears to be a penny short of a pound if anyone were to ask me. So, naturally, I doubted her. Yet here you are." Tilly shrugged. "Seems she was right. I can scarcely countenance it."

Despite Kate's cheeks warming with embarrassment, she still stared in disbelief at her sister's nonchalant materialization from the dark, terrifying crevices Kate had imagined. Then she noticed Aunt Honore's lady's maid, Lorraine, standing behind and off to Tilly's side.

Clockwork cogs turned feverishly in Kate's head. It only took a moment to deduce what her wicked, horrible, despicable aunt had known all along—

Tilly had NOT been lost.

Her little sister yammered on. "I've been to the Royal Menagerie, Katie. You really must see it! They have one gigantic African lion and two tigers."

Not lost at all.

"If you ask me, the tigers are much scarier than the lion— all that orange and black is quite fearsome. Luckily, they're all behind bars. Not too happy about it, though. One of the tigers growled at me. Don't look so worried, Katie. I jumped back when it pawed the iron bars." Tilly leaned closer, and her eyes widened as she confided, "But I do think that tiger would've eaten me, if she could."

Kate stared tight-lipped as Tilly continued her story.

"You would be proud of me. I didn't run away like a baby.

I stood my ground and let her growl at me. She roared! Leaping and charging as if she wanted to rip my liver to pieces." Tilly waved the lollipop around, describing the encounter. "I did what you do, Katie. I gritted my teeth and clenched my fists and told her 'bad kitty.'"

Tilly beamed, waiting for approval, as if withstanding that roar had been her chief accomplishment in life. When no approbation came forth, she licked her lollipop again. "After that, Lorraine pulled me away. Oh, but the very best animal in the whole menagerie is the elephant! You never saw anything so enormous in your whole life. It's the size of four horses put together—unless you count Papa's Norwegian workhorse, then it's maybe only as big as three of those."

Speechless, Kate gaped at Tilly, a dozen emotions tumbling in different directions. Finally, she gave up trying to land on one and grabbed Tilly up into a fierce hug. "We thought you were lost!"

Greyson closed in around them and patted Tilly's back affectionately. "Thank goodness you are all right."

"Of course I'm all right." Tilly thumped Katie's shoulder. "Put me down, Katie. Your hair is getting stuck on my lollipop."

Setting her back on her feet, Kate bent down to chasten her baby sister. "Why did you leave without telling anyone?"

"You were asleep." Tilly sniffed as if it were of no importance. "Anyway, Aunt Honore ordered me to go away and stop asking so many annoying questions. She told me to take her maid and visit a sweet shop, or go feed squirrels in the park. What fidget-headed person would feed squirrels? I tried to explain no one from Clapsforth-on-Wye would do that. People where I come from have enough sense to know squirrels are quite capable of feeding themselves. Our aunt didn't care. She told me to go somewhere, *anywhere*, but stop bothering her."

Kate crossed her arms and frowned. "And so you decided to traipse off to the menagerie?"

"No." Tilly rubbed her arm. "I was about to go up to our room, but Aunt Honore grabbed my arm. *On second thought,* says she, I insist you visit the Royal Menagerie and pay particular attention to the monkey cage. Notice how aggravating their constant racket is—because I intend to lock you in a similar cage if you don't stop pestering me." Tilly imitated Aunt Honore's irritated voice and mimicked their aunt's favorite shooing motion.

Kate narrowed her gaze at Lorraine, who stood primly off to the side looking at passing carriages, a banal expression masking her features. "My aunt sent you on this escapade, didn't she?"

Lorraine sniffed haughtily. "I never question my lady's requests, miss. 'Tis my duty to obey, naught else."

"Hhmm, I see." Kate wrapped a protective arm around Tilly. "Well, thank you for at least keeping her safe."

At that, Lorraine reanimated. "Oh miss, those tigers was ferocious. Shook me to the bone, they did. Miss Matilda didn't budge an inch. Your wee little lass stood there, brave as brave can be. I never seen anything like it."

"I doubt those tigers are any more dangerous than my devious aunt," muttered Kate. She leaned down to Tilly, and in the clearest, calmest voice she could muster, asked, "Are you quite certain Aunt Honore knew where you were going?"

"Oh, yes. Aunt Honore gave Lorraine a bag of coins and told her *to keep the bothersome brat away as long as possible.* By 'bothersome brat,' naturally she meant me. We even had enough money left over to buy tea for Lorraine and this sweet for me." Tilly grinned proudly.

Kate patted her sister's shoulder. "You are not a bothersome brat, my love."

"Sometimes I am."

"Sometimes we all are." Kate smiled and leaned closer to whisper, "But I do believe our Aunt Honore is the biggest brat of all."

And the woman must pay for her deceit.

Chapter 21
Bringing Down Auntie

KATE SNATCHED UP Tilly's hand. "Come along." Without turning to see if Greyson or Lorraine followed, she marched up the street ready to do battle with the dragon of Alison Hall.

She intended to put paid to Aunt Honore's machinations once and for all. What had possessed the woman to trick Kate into thinking dear sweet innocent little Tilly was lost and wandering the streets of London. The woman was a raving lunatic . . .

A *ruinous* . . .

conniving . . .

madwoman!

"Argh!" rumbled unbidden from her throat.

Greyson kept pace with her. "Now, Katie, you're getting much too upset."

Tilly was dragging her feet. And somewhere behind them, the maid, Lorraine, clip-clopped grumpily. "Yes, miss. Do slow down. You're making a scene."

"I don't care," Kate said to Greyson, not the maid. "My aunt spoils everything." *Everything.*

Case in point, she and Greyson had just been about to kiss when all this happened. Kate issued a warning growl, just the way Ralphie did when annoyed. "All I can say is, Aunt Honore better be wearing a cast-iron corset because I plan to run her through with the nearest umbrella."

Tilly planted her feet. "Don't be daft, Katie. You can't run anyone through with an umbrella."

Kate yanked her sister back into a vigorous trot. "Yes, I can. Just watch me."

"I s'pose you might try beating her over the head with one." Tilly practiced a whacking motion with her candy.

That murderous thought danced merrily in Kate's mind for two entire blocks. But the more she considered it, the more she realized what Lady Alameda needed was a sound spanking. If only there'd been a willow tree on the way back, Kate might've cut a switch to do the job properly.

Too late for that.

As it was, all four of them stood on the front step of Aunt Honore's townhouse. *Weaponless.* Before she even had a chance to knock, Cairn opened the door with his customary stoicism.

With a fortifying breath, Kate strode in, ready to summon her dastardly aunt by roaring at the top of her lungs.

Except there was no need.

Lady Alameda stood in the center of the foyer, tranquil as a sugared daisy. Nora stood on one side of their aunt and Sadie on the other. Honore stepped forward. "Ah! There you are. See, I told you Matilda would be fine, didn't I? And here she is, not a scratch on her."

Some of the wind left Kate's admittedly ragged sails. Still, she managed a stern, "How could you?"

"How could I, *what*?"

"Do such a thing."

"By *thing*, do you mean arrange a situation that served your best interest?"

"My best interest!? Not ruddy likely. You were meddling! Playing the puppeteer, entertaining yourself at my expense. You couldn't possibly know what is best for me."

"Are you, or are you not, re-engaged to this young man?" She gestured at Lord Colter.

"I—I, that is to say, I believe we may have reached an understanding." She glanced shyly up at him.

He cleared his throat. "I, uh . . . *yes*. Or so I thought." He squinted warily at Kate.

"Ha! I knew it. See there." Honore crossed her arms smugly. "That proves my point. I am an excellent judge of what's best for you and your pack of unruly sisters."

Kate frowned, her mind a jumbled storm, and after blustering incoherently for a few seconds, blurted, "Nora is not *unruly*."

"Isn't she? I believe you have miscalculated in her regard, too. Nora is as headstrong as the rest of you. Obviously, you don't understand them, or yourself, as well as you think you do. As for my knowing what's best for *you*, even a child could have deduced that you and this fellow belong together."

"A child? That's preposterous."

"Not at all." Honore stooped slightly and crooked her finger at Tilly. "Matilda, my dear, were you, or were you not, quite certain that Lord Colter was the exact right match for your sister?"

Tilly's face opened as a flower does to the sun. "You're asking my opinion? Truly?"

"Yes, darling, I am." Honore's tone resonated with sugary earnestness.

Tilly straightened to her full height. "Yes. I knew it from the start."

Impossible.

Kate had never been sure of their relationship until the last few days. And Greyson, well, the entire village had witnessed his doubts. She shook her head. "You couldn't have."

"I did," Tilly bristled, her little hands turning to fists despite the sweet still clutched in one. She stamped her foot. "I knew because Lord Colter cared about all of us!" She frowned ferociously at Katie. "He wouldn't have put up with all of us if he didn't love you—really, truly love you—would he? He wasn't just another gentleman thinking you were beautiful."

"*Beautiful.*" Katie let out an exasperated puff of air. "What utter nonsense. *That* was never a problem."

"Don't be thick!" Sadie huffed. "It would've been if Lord Colter hadn't run them all off."

"What?" Kate drew back. "He never did—" Except he was turning his eyes up to the ceiling and stretching his neck as if his nonexistent cravat was too tight. Her mouth dropped open. "You didn't?"

Sadie crossed her arms, mimicking their obnoxious aunt. "Of course he did. Don't tell me you are unaware of Sir Plimpton's son, Matthew? He practically drools every time you walk past him. And Fredrick Peterson—surely you remember him stumbling over his feet rushing to ask you to dance at the Harvest Ball? What of Jeremy Ellis? Or George Oates?" She ticked them off on her fingers. "For pity's sake, Katie. Are you completely blind? Even the vicar was swoony over you—poor fellow is obviously in want of a wife. Haven't you noticed how he blushes bright pink every Sunday when you thank him for his sermon? If Lord Colter hadn't warned them all off, you'd have had a dozen suitors banging at our door. And not one of them half so right for you as he is." Sadie swung her palm in Lord Colter's direction.

Kate squinted, trying to remember the other young men in their village. Had they truly paid her any special attention?

Surely not.

Except . . .

She swallowed. They had. Somewhere in the back of her mind, she'd noticed, the same way one scarcely pays notice to a bee flying past or a bird twittering overhead. She simply hadn't cared about any of them—only Greyson.

She sighed and stared at her fingers folded tightly as if in earnest prayer, although she'd initially clamped them together to keep from strangling her wicked aunt.

"There you are. *Proof!*" Honore's strident voice softened minimally. "I simply helped you see what everyone else already knew."

Perhaps.

Even so, the woman's methods were completely unacceptable. "You were cruel! It was heartless to make me to think Tilly was lost. It laid a terror on me."

"A terror? Ha! You? Fiddlesticks." Honore's tone turned caustic again. "Nothing terrifies you, except marriage. Aside from that, as I told you before, this child—" She jabbed a finger at Tilly who stood idly by licking her annoyingly cheerful lollipop. "—is more than capable of taking care of herself. *However*, anticipating you would throw this silly tantrum, I assigned my most trusted servant to watch over her. Did I not?"

She did.

Kate unpinched her lips and drew in a deep, calming breath. "Be that as it may, my sisters and I shall be leaving first thing in the morning. I intend to hire a coach for our journey back to Clapsforth-on-Wye."

Nora shook her head. "No, I'm afraid that won't be—"

"What! Leave?" Sophie interrupted, stomping her foot. "No! We can't. It's too soon. I haven't attended one single ball, or—"

Outside a coach clattered loudly in front of the house, and everyone started clamoring at her all at once. Kate fought the urge to clamp her hands over her ears.

Greyson stood next to her, insisting she needn't rent a coach. "I shall provide suitable conveyance."

Tilly nattered on about wanting to take one more trip to the sweet shop before leaving.

"Hush! All of you, hush!" Lady Alameda clapped her hands. "Stop kicking up such a fuss, Kate. I insist you stay here and enjoy the rest of the season."

Thump! Thump-thump!

Loud pounding on the front door silenced them all.

The butler, Cairn, seemed to materialize out of nowhere and opened to the caller. There stood a large man in a caped greatcoat, his silhouette filling the door frame, fist raised to continue knocking.

"Papa?" Kate blinked in disbelief.

"Papa!" Tilly's shout echoed through the marble hall. She ran and threw her arms around their father.

Like a flock of ducklings, they all floated toward him. He jostled his way into the foyer with Tilly still clinging to his waist. Sadie began prattling, "Have you come to stay for the season? Now that you're here, you must talk some sense into Katie and our aunt. They won't allow me to attend—"

"Father, how good of you to come." Nora's calm voice pleasantly hushed Sadie. She helped him out of his greatcoat.

He handed his hat to Cairn.

"Yes, Cavendish." Honore stood back near the staircase,

arms folded, lips pressed in a surly pout. "Why have you come?"

"Overdue, I expect." He patted Sadie on the head, but addressed his sister. "Truth be told, I was somewhat surprised I hadn't heard from you a few days ago. Figured by now my little scamps would've driven you right over the precipice."

"Nothing I can't manage." Honore hoisted her chin higher.

"Us?" Kate couldn't keep her voice level. "Driven *her* over the edge?" Outrage rammed it up another octave. "It is quite the other way around, I assure you. Why, only today, she—"

"Solved an enormous family problem." Lady Alameda donned a superior air and gestured to Lord Colter. "This gentleman and your daughter have reconciled their differences. Isn't that so, Kate, darling?"

Aunt Honore ought to have been born a queen. She certainly commanded a regal air that gave pause to those about to defy her. "I . . . well, yes . . . That is to say . . ."

How could Kate spill the truth to her father, here, now, in front of everyone?

She couldn't very well confess publicly that she had only recently realized she loved Greyson. Nor could she admit that she now treasured her sisters even though looking after them sometimes made her feel trapped.

No.

She could not.

Yet she needed to explain to him somehow. *But how?* Her thoughts crashed together in a thundering storm of confusion, and without any rhyme or reason, words poured from her lips in an incoherent flood. "Oh, Papa. I do love Lord Colter. I do! And Aunt Honore *did* help a tiny bit but in such a mean, *awful* manner. She made me think our little Tilly was *lost*." She shook her head trying to banish the thought. "It was terrible."

Aunt Honore protested but Kate paid no heed. "Except Tilly wasn't really lost, and then I wanted to strangle Aunt Honore. Or wallop her with an umbrella. And now I don't want to do that, except maybe I still do a little." She snuffled. "Now that you're here, I wouldn't do such a thing, of course."

Honore sputtered some nonsense about daring her to try.

Kate leaned into her father's shoulder, burying her face in the sturdy weave of his coat. "How did you know we needed you, Papa? I wish you would've come sooner—not that we *did* need you. What I mean to say is, I could've managed on my own. Really, I could have. And I was about to rent a carriage and bring us all home. We can't stay here with her; it's too chaotic. I don't know which way is up around her. Why *did* you come? I'm so very glad that you did, but—"

She was blubbering.

Miss Kate Linnet, the young lady with the iron backbone, was sobbing and dripping tears like a lost child.

"Katie, Katie." Father patted her shoulders and held her while she cried. "Of course you could've managed. You always do. Not that I should've left it to you. You're too capable, my dear. That's your problem. Never should've allowed you to carry so much on your wee shoulders."

Shouldn't you have?

He clasped those shoulders and forced her to look at him. "They are *my* daughters, not yours. My responsibilities. Do you hear me, Katie, girl?"

Clouds parted, and her heart sailed free for the first time in years.

She nodded.

"Good. That's my girl." He gave her a gentle pat. "Didn't realize till the house stood empty as a tomb how much I missed you all." He smiled at the four of them. "You're my poppets!" He chucked Sadie under the chin. "Mine. Do ye hear? And I've come to take you all home where you belong. You've my thanks for bringing them to town, Honore. But we'll be going back to Clapsforth-on-Wye in the morning."

He leaned in to study Kate. "Unless, my girl, you'd prefer to stay in London to be near your fiancé? You *are* engaged again, are you not?" He turned to Lord Colter for confirmation, who turned to Kate and waited, consternation and hope dancing a wild jig on his face.

She stepped away from her father and turned watery eyes up to Greyson. "I would rather return home. There is much preparation to be made. That is, Lord Colter, if you are still of a mind to—"

"If?" Greyson grabbed her hands. "You're ready to marry me now?"

She smiled at the delight in his face, and reached up to smooth her hand over his dear, bruised cheek. "Yes. I can think of no place I would rather be than at your side through all the troubles that are sure to come *and* the happiness. Yes."

Hope won the dance on his features.

Greyson kissed her.

Right there in front of everyone. Not a chaste peck. He covered her mouth with his, and warmth flowed into her, bathing away her heart's bruises, melting her worries, caressing her wounded soul. She felt a oneness with him that she knew, without a doubt, would outlast any storm.

So, naturally, she kissed him again and this time even more fervently.

"Ahem." Father cleared his throat.

Aunt Honore was not so delicate. "If you do not stop that this instant, young man, I will be forced to find my pistol and demand you get a special license. Not to mention, Kate, your sisters are attending far too closely the mechanics of . . . er . . . your lovemaking."

They broke apart, and Kate hid her reddened lips with her fingers. "I-I'm sorry."

"Don't be." Sadie grinned perniciously. "It looked perfectly divine to me."

Aunt Honore flicked Sadie's arm. "You're going to have no end of problems with this one, brother dearest."

Undoubtedly.

Tilly cocked her head. "Why all the fuss? They were only kissing. It's not as if—"

"Yes, darling. They were merely kissing." Nora bent down, distracting Tilly. "This remarkable sweet of yours looks quite delectable."

"Not as delectable as *merely* kissing," muttered Sadie.

Kate's cheeks flushed with heat and Greyson stifled a laugh.

Merely kissing?

It seemed so much more than that. Bonding. Promising. Unifying. Their kisses seemed to embody a thousand other things. *Pleasant things.*

Having distracted Tilly, Nora reached for Kate's hand and held it in both of hers. "Kate, dearest. I'm so happy for you. You must write to me the moment you set the wedding date."

"Write to you?" Kate blinked, not understanding.

"Yes. I shall be remaining here with our aunt."

"Here? No. No!" Kate shook her head. "You can't. Papa, you can't let her stay. It isn't safe. Lady Alameda isn't a suitable guardian. She's—"

"You mustn't worry. I am well aware of our aunt's propensity for mischief." Nora waited patiently until Kate could breathe normally before continuing. "Lady Alameda has invited me to stay on as her protégé."

"Her protégé? Oh no, Nora, darling, she doesn't mean it. It is simply her way of manipulating—"

"Humph!" Honore grumbled loudly. "I *do* mean it. I have finally found the one niece capable of taking her place beside me in society."

Kate turned, pleading with her aunt. "Dear, sweet Nora? Surely not."

"Once again, my dear, you have underestimated your sister. Did you not observe how deftly she orchestrated coming along with you this season? How masterfully she handled that rogue Lord Weatherford?"

Greyson grumbled at the mention of that gentleman.

Honore continued to list Nora's accomplishments. "You saw, didn't you, how the young men gathered around her at Almack's, offering her glasses of punch, holding her fan, vying with one another for the honor of walking her out onto the dance floor? Perhaps you failed to notice the hothouse bouquets littering my sitting room."

It was true. Nora seemed to have cast a spell over the gentlemen of London. But as extraordinary as Nora might be, she was still Kate's sister and needed protection. "Yes, Nora is remarkable. An angel. Whereas you—you're a ... a ..."

"Not an angel." Honore supplied in the nick of time. "Exactly. We are equally matched opposites."

"That is hardly a commendation." Kate tugged on her father's sleeve. "Papa, surely you can't think this is proper?"

"Hhmm. Wouldn't have thought so. But now that I consider it, I see my sister makes a fair point."

"No! Surely not." Kate's chest tightened up and her pulse thundered in her ears. "I won't be here to protect her."

"Now, Kathryn," Father said, employing her full name, which brought her racing thoughts to a halt, "Nora is a remarkably capable young woman. You've taught her well." He patted her arm. "Think on it, my girl. You know full well that none of the young men at home are suitable matches for her. Much as we will miss her, there comes a time when all birds must learn to fly on their own."

"Daresay Nora's been flapping quite efficiently for several years." This bothersome bit of wisdom issued forth from Sadie's mouth. At Kate's scolding frown, her stubborn sister added, "She keeps us in line well enough when you're not looking. And what's more, I want to stay here, too."

"No," Papa said flatly. "Nora may remain here with my sister, but the rest of you are coming home, and there's an end to the matter."

Nora clasped Kate's hands. "Do you trust me, Kate?"

She did. Then why did it feel as if a vital organ were being torn from her body? Her heart beat in grievous thuds and she could barely speak. "Yes. But I will miss you."

"And I, you," Nora said, as if she knew exactly how much it hurt.

Nora, the one sister Kate could count on, the steadying influence. The thought of not having her close stung. She groped for the right thing to say. "I—I—"

"You'll be fine." There it was: Nora's soothing voice, washing over her like a lullaby. Oh, how she would miss her. Then Kate felt Greyson's protective nearness and that made her feel a trifle stronger.

She forced a smile. "No doubt you will be the belle of the season. Even so, you must not rely upon our aunt. She is—"

"A delightful challenge." Nora grinned.

"See there." Lady Alameda chortled mischievously. "I'm a *delightful challenge.*"

A notorious rascal.

Kate focused a searing glare upon her rascally aunt. "If anything untoward happens to my sister, I shall come back and run you through with an umbrella." Not waiting for a reply from her aunt, she turned back to Nora. "You must promise to take good care of yourself."

"I do. And no matter what happens, you always have my love. For now, though, our paths must diverge." Nora embraced Kate and a gentle strength flowed between them, tying them together forever, sister to sister, a bond stronger than hammered steel. "It is time to see what adventures lie ahead for me."

When they pulled apart and stood face to face, Kate wondered how she could have been blind all these years to the raw power that seemed to emanate from Nora. She took a deep breath and turned to Honore. "I do believe, Aunt, you may be outmatched."

Kate meant every word.

—Epilogue—
Rose Petals

THE YOUNG VICAR of Clapsforth-on-Wye hurried in their direction, and his eyes widened when he saw Kate and Greyson pinning their banns to the church wall. The forlorn expression he donned embarrassed Kate for his sake.

"Are you truly certain?" he asked plaintively. "Marriage is a momentous decision, a lifelong—"

"Yes! Yes, we are," Lord Colter hastened to assure him.

The vicar ignored Greyson, waiting attentively for Kate's response. "'Tis a lifelong commitment. You ought to be absolutely sure."

"Yes, I am quite certain," she answered. "Lord Colter is dearer to me than I ever could have imagined. I'm exceedingly happy." Admitting it to their parson, she could not keep joy from bubbling up into a broad smile. "We would be most pleased if you would agree to perform the ceremony. Oh, do say you will."

His countenance seemed to sag into the black depths of his cassock, but he nodded. "Of course." He sighed and smiled feebly. "If that is your wish."

That Sunday morning, the vicar stood in the pulpit and read their banns aloud in a very pinched manner, his neck turning a vivid shade of pink. His announcement of her intended union with Lord Colter stirred members of the congregation like a north wind. They murmured with disbelief. Several turned to peer at Kate and Lord Colter. Others shrugged and shook their heads.

By the third Sunday, to Kate's great relief, the vicar read the banns with commendable fortitude. Parishioners listened without murmurs or gasps this time, although Kate noticed some of them exchanging winks and knowing nods.

She maintained a steely posture. *Let them think what they will.* She and Lord Colter would weather their disapproval, and in time their neighbors would forget and move on to some fresh scandal.

In pure defiance of the villager's petty gossip, the very next Wednesday, wearing the regal ballgown Aunt Honore had given her, Kate strode into the Assembly Ball. Primed to brave their criticism, her hand rested gracefully on Greyson's arm. She fixed her chin at a proper angle—not too high and proud, nor too low and timid.

A hush fell over the room as they entered.

Steady on.

The next moment, to her utter amazement, everyone in attendance sprang to their feet. *Huzzahs* and *felicitations* peppered the air. Villagers seemed to be clapping with delight.

She glanced right and left in amazement.

Smiles.

Everywhere she looked, friends and neighbors were smiling. Kate's cheeks flushed with heat, and she leaned unsteadily on his arm, not quite sure what to think.

Were they truly wishing her happiness?

Lady Plimpton, an enormous ostrich feather sprouting from her somewhat archaic but highly pouffed and powdered coiffure, glided toward them. "There you are, my dear girl. And *Lord Colter.*" She bobbed a curtsy to them both. "Always a delight. We wondered when you would pay us a visit."

Mrs. Oates, three blue and green peacock feathers swaying precariously in her hair, scurried up behind Lady Plimpton and exclaimed, "What a perfectly stunning gown."

Four more ladies gathered around them, all chattering at once. Greyson lifted an eyebrow. "I believe I shall make myself useful and procure some punch. *Ladies.*" He bowed and made his escape.

Kate felt trapped by a flock of oversized birds. Feathers of various colors and sizes fluttered before her face.

"Ahem," Lady Plimpton silenced the ladies and commanded their attention. "We, the Clapsforth-on-Wye Ladies Society, would like to host your wedding breakfast."

"Yes." Mrs. Blumsbury's chin protruded resolutely, as if

they would brook no argument. "That's right."

"Oh, but you needn't go to all that trouble," Kate protested. "I can manage. 'Twill be naught but a small affair, surely."

Silence ensued. The feathers all cocked awkwardly in Lady Plimpton's direction. She exhaled through a pinched nose and responded for them all. "Of course you can, dear. We've all observed how you managed your sisters over the years."

They nodded, feathers bobbing in unison.

"Anyone else would've asked for help." Mrs. Oates's tone didn't sound wholly complimentary.

"But not you." Mrs. Peterson sniffed.

"No." Mrs. Ellis shook her head mournfully. "Not her."

"We offered." Mrs. Blumsbury's chin went up. "More'n once." Then her gaze dropped to the tip of her silk slippers. "We wanted to help. All of us missed your ma, you know."

Kate felt as if she were being scolded. "I thought . . ."

What had she thought?

That she was alone.

"I didn't know . . ."

"Time passed, and you seemed quite capable." Lady Plimpton rapped her fan in her palm. "Mistakes on both sides—I'm sure. Water under bygone bridges, my dear. Gone. Done." Lady Plimpton waved Kate's protests away. "This time, however, we will not be deterred. *Everyone* in the village wishes to celebrate your and Lord Colter's forthcoming wedding. Surely you will not deny us that?"

Deny them?

Kate blinked in confusion. "No, of course not."

"Good! Then it's settled." Mrs. Peterson's pink feathers jiggled wildly as she clapped her gloved hands. "My husband says we may hold the wedding breakfast here in the Assembly Hall. We'll all walk straight over from the church."

"Perfect!" Mrs. Oates exclaimed. "And I spoke with Mr. Mott at the bakery just yesterday. He assured me he'll bake plenty of rolls and make us a fine currant and brandy bride cake with almond frosting. Won't that be a treat!"

Mrs. Plimpton nodded her approval. "Excellent. Sir Plimpton and I shall supply a roast pig with enough ham and bacon for everyone in the village. 'Tis a day worth celebrating. A day we all hoped and prayed for, but. . ." She sighed, hefting one eyebrow as if Lord Colter's outburst at that fateful assembly might have been Kate's doing. "We despaired it might never come. Yet here it is, a joyous miracle for all of us to share."

"We'll have flowers and fiddlers playing, and everyone will dance and sing songs." Mrs. Blumsbury dabbed at her rheumy eyes. "A right proper celebration."

"Aye," Mrs. Ellis agreed and grasped Kate's forearm. "Your dear mother is sure to be watching from above—I just know it—and she'll be singing with us."

They spoke so tenderly of her mother that Kate could scarcely answer. She nodded happily at all their suggestions, and for the first time in ten years, she didn't feel alone and motherless.

Greyson finally extracted her for the one and only waltz

of the night, and asked her why she looked so radiant. She answered with a full heart. "I love you, Greyson. I love Clapsforth-on-Wye. I love my sisters and my father. I'm having one of those moments you promised me—a wondrous gift of joy."

The very next morning, a parcel arrived from London. It contained a letter from Nora and, surprisingly, a gift from Aunt Honore—a stunning dress designed by the brilliant Madame Brigitte. The gown fit Kate to perfection, accenting her curves in all the right places. She had been content to be married in her best ballgown, but this was exquisite—a watered gold silk gown, trimmed with pearls, with a white tulle train. She could never have afforded a garment of this quality. She twirled in front of the mirror and thought for a moment that she looked like a Roman princess.

"Very pretty," Sadie admitted reluctantly. "I hope Aunt Honore takes me to London when she tires of Nora."

"Nora sent a letter." Kate felt guilty keeping it to herself. She intended to share it after she'd read it for herself a few times. "She and our Aunt Honore will arrive in two days' time."

"That's cutting it close. The wedding is the very next day."

"Yes, and apparently, our Nora has a duke in tow. He is accompanying them as a guest."

"A duke!" Sadie sprang up from her chair. "Coming here?"

"That's what it says."

"But we aren't ready. The house is—"

"A disaster. Yes, I know." Kate held the letter out to her sister to read. "She says it's of no consequence, and not to make a fuss. *Let him to see us as we are*, she says. And so that is what we will do."

"A duke." Sadie flopped down on Kate's bed. "That means our Nora is to be a duchess."

"Don't count duke-lings before they're hatched," Kate chuckled.

Sadie groaned. "That's not even remotely humorous."

"Fussbudget." Kate snatched the letter back. "I doubt she likes him very much. Her note doesn't sound very eager about the prospect." Kate tried to unbutton her gown to no avail. "Can you please help me out of this?"

Sadie unbuttoned the pearl closures on the back of the bodice. "Well, I'll take him if she won't."

"Don't say such things. You will mind your manners, young lady," Kate warned sternly.

"Where's the fun in that?"

It was Kate's turn to groan.

Later that afternoon, she and Greyson sat in the garden swing that Papa had built for the girls. It was wide enough and had a sturdy enough back that it could accommodate all four of them when they were little.

"Nora's bringing a duke, huh?" he toyed with Kate's

fingers clasped in his.

"So she says."

"Aiming high, I suppose." He kissed the back of her palm.

"I suppose. Her letter was rather cryptic." A butterfly fluttered past, twirling upside down in the breeze.

Greyson sat up a bit and sounded suddenly serious. "Do you wish you had a duke in tow?"

"Not a bit of it." She leaned her head on his shoulder watching Ralphie stalk rabbits and gallop after Tilly, who was weaving in and out among the roses. "Do you wish you had a duchess on your shoulder?"

"A duchess? Hhhmm. Well, let me think—"

She rapped his arm. He leaned into her. "Unless *you* were that duchess, my love, I wouldn't have the slightest interest."

She grinned.

Tilly skipped toward them, Ralphie trotting at her heels and a basket in her hand. "Look, Katie! Rose petals to throw at your wedding." She thrust out her basket brimming with pink, red, and white rose petals.

"Where did you find so many? I thought I'd cut off most—" She caught herself before admitting to having murdered so many roses. "Um . . . I didn't think there were that many blooms left."

"That's the thing with roses." Tilly raised aloft the loaded basket. "You can lop them off, but they come back stronger than ever."

A gust danced through the garden, whirling a cloud of Tilly's roses into the air, showering silky petals over Kate and

Greyson. As the blossoms fell against her cheeks and landed in her hair, Kate leaned back against his chest, laughing.

And treasured the moment in her heart.

My Dear Reader,

DID YOU ENJOY Kate's journey to finding love and a way forward with Lord Colter? I hope so.

I love the idea of keeping a keen watch for those blessed golden moments in our everyday lives. Often, I have looked back on my difficulties and struggles and been surprised to discover those dark times held some of my most valuable experiences, bleak moments filled with hidden treasures. I hope your troubles may be few and that those you do experience will reveal their treasures as time passes.

FYI, I took artistic license in the scene with the doctor sewing up Greyson's wound. Sterilization procedures that we take for granted did not come into general medical practices use for another few years. I like to think that Kate would've had commonsense enough to think the needle should be clean.

For more about medical practices during the Regency era, and, (if you have the stomach for it,) a look at some of their actual surgical equipment, visit the Historical Extras page on my website: KathleenBaldwin.com

If you enjoyed reading this book, **please _lend_ your copy** to a friend, _recommend_ it to your book club, or _write a review_! Reviews help other readers discover your favorite books. If you write one for _The Persuasion of Miss Kate_, please let me know. I would like to thank you personally.

Email: Kathleen@KathleenBaldwin.com

JOIN Kathleen's Tea Time Newsletter!

New subscribers receive a gift of an eBook in the welcome note. You'll also get exclusive short stories, insider info, sneak peeks, contest scoops, free eBooks, and other fun tidbits.

Please Note: Kathleen's newsletter only comes out a few times a year. Be sure to whitelist her or add her email address to your contacts so that you don't miss out on the fun.

https://KathleenBaldwin.com/newsletter-subscription/

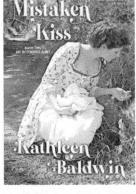

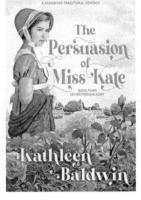

AWARD-WINNING
BESTSELLING SERIES

ENJOYED BY MORE THAN
500,000 READERS
WORLD-WIDE

What critics say about the Stranje House Novels

"Sign me up for Kathleen Baldwin's *School for Unusual Girls*. It sucked me in from the first few pages and kept me reading until late into the night." —**Meg Cabot**, #1 NYT-USA *Today* bestselling author of *The Princess Diaries*

"A *School for Unusual Girls* by Kathleen Baldwin is enticing from the first sentence . . . Baldwin has an ear for period dialogue as she draws us into this world of sharp, smart young ladies who are actually being trained and deployed for the British war effort by the mysterious head-mistress, Miss Stranje. It's speculative historical fiction, with a trace of steampunk inventiveness."
— ***New York Times Sunday Book Review***

"Spellbinding! A *School for Unusual Girls* is a beautifully written tale that will appeal to every girl who has ever felt different . . . a true page-turner!"
–**Lorraine Heath**, NYT-USA *Today* bestselling author

"I enjoyed this story immensely and I closed my kindle with a satisfied sigh." —**YA *Insider***

"Baldwin has a winning series here: her characters are intriguing and fully rendered." —**Booklist**

"Refuge for Masterminds moves at a fast pace from the first page and doesn't stop. Although it is written with a young adult audience in mind, it is a fun and enjoyable novel and will also appeal to adult readers." —**Historical Novel Society**

"I am in love with the Stranje House novels. Seriously, in love."
—**Book Briefs**

The Stranje House Novels

"Enticing from the first sentence" – *New York Times Sunday Book Review*

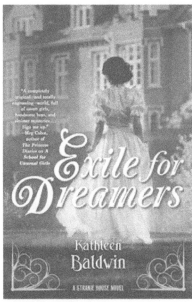

A girl's spy school set amidst Jane Austen's High Society

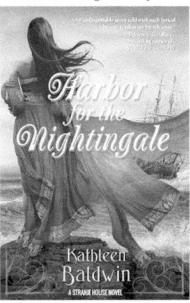